GIFT OF THE
RAVEN

CATRIONA
TROTH

TRISKELE BOOKS

Published by Piebald Publishing

piebald.publishing@gmail.com

ISBN: 978-0-9576180-1-5

To my mum and dad, who turned me into a New Canadian, and then had the patience and forbearance to let me turn myself back into an Old European.

Acknowledgements

I have so many people to be grateful to, both at Triskele Books and at the amazing sanctuary that is the Writing Asylum. Between them, they have provided the perfect blend of moral support and incisive editing advice. Special thanks must go to Amanda Hodgkinson for wielding her editorial knife with such grace and skill, to Jane Dixon Smith for her brilliant cover design and to Perry Iles for his keen eye for errors and other infelicities.

PART I

1959-1965

Chapter 1

For years, my den was the only safe place.

All that time, the bad time, runs together in my mind, but I reckon I was about eight or nine when I found it. I was running, trying to get as far away as possible, pain hog-tying me. And I fell, bum first. Between the line of bush that straggled round the edge of the park and the first of the tall trees, my feet found empty air. When I hit the ground, I broke into a million pieces. Then I looked up at the roof of saplings that closed over my head and knew for sure: no one was gonna find me here.

After that I'd come up whenever I could sneak away. That bit of the park was where families came for their picnics. Every Sunday from Victoria Day through to Labour Day—longer in a good summer. They'd kick off their shoes, pull their shirts over their heads, show off their pale skins. Some of them'd cook on the rusted old metal barbecue. I liked that. Afterwards I'd take charcoal from their fires. It was crap to draw with but it was better than nothing. I drew on the backs of envelopes I swiped from the trash. Pictures of my dad and me, mostly. In a canoe. Shooting a bow.

For a few stolen hours, I was the Hunter, and I stalked the families.

The birds could see me there, and the little brown mice that lived in the roots of the trees. But the kids, the moms and dads—they hadn't a clue. They thought they were safe. Eating their hotdogs. Playing ball. Dads coaching their sons. *Play ball! A jeu!*

My dad would've taught me different stuff. If he'd been here. Not throwing and catching. But hunting. Shooting. How to put an arrow right between their blue eyes. How to scalp them. But Dad had to go away, long time ago. I had to teach myself, from books and that. Make him proud of me, so he'd come back.

The nearest anyone ever came to finding me was this one time when a family was playing softball right below the woods. Mom, dad, two boys and a little girl. All pale skinned and golden haired. Burnt up a little in the sun. Shouting to each other so that you could have heard them away down the other side of the park.

One of the boys swung the bat wildly, and the softball came crashing through the trees. Two blue jays, mad as hell, flew overhead shouting, *go on, get away!* The ball bounced once at the lip of my hollow. An explosion of dust blew up from the dry earth and the ball rolled down into the den.

Once again, my body was stiff and sore. I had to force my hand along, groping over the dry earth till I made contact with a hard, round lump that rolled a little as I touched it. I curled my fingers around the seam and pushed the ball out as far as I could along the edge of the hollow, onto a patch of open ground.

The small kid saw it first. I saw his t-shirt, red like a cardinal, zigzagging through the trees and heard his cry of triumph. He homed in on the ball, his running shoes trampling the underbrush. His arm was skinny and freckled and covered in golden hairs just beginning to grow. It almost touched my head. I thought about grabbing it, pulling him down into the hollow with me, silencing his racket. Then his mom called.

'Jonathan? You got it?'

'Yeah, Mom. I got it.' His voice was high and squeaky. I saw the bottoms of his runners as he turned to go. His mom was waiting for him and he ran to her, holding the ball up high. At the edge of the woods, they hugged, their arms tight round each other, the mom's hands in the small of his back.

My mom never hugged me like that. Leastways, not for a long time.

She did once. I'm almost sure of it. Back when we still lived with Auntie Jean. Before Ed came and took us away.

One of the first things I remember is squatting on the grass in Auntie Jean's backyard, making patterns with wax crayons on a sheet of paper. I move my hand, and colour trails out behind the crayon. I haven't exactly figured how it happens, but it fascinates me.

Inside, Auntie Jean, her face red, scrubs the kitchen one more time between breakfast and lunch. Auntie Flora, on her way from here to there, talks to her through the window. Mom lies asleep on a lawn chair under the maple tree, the blue flowers on her dress tumbling out of her lap and onto the grass.

I want to kiss her; so I get up and toddle towards her. But before I get there, I'm spotted.

'Don't let him wake her, Flora,' calls Auntie Jean.

Flora comes dancing down off the porch and scoops me up. 'Let her sleep a bit longer, sweetie.' She waltzes me in slow, wide circles round the garden, singing softly:

> *I am a man upon land,*
> *I'm a selkie on the sea,*
> *And when I'm far frae every strand,*
> *My dwelling is in Sule Skerry.*

I hold onto handfuls of her hair in my fists. It is red, like a sunset. Mom's hair, tied back in a broad blue ribbon, is gold like noonday. Even Auntie Jean's hair, pulled away from her face in a tight little bun, is pale like morning. My hair is black like night, and my skin is the colour of Auntie Jean's strong tea. I've never seen anyone who looks like me but that's okay, 'cos I belong here anyway.

At last we come to a halt by the porch. Auntie Jean, frowning mightily at both of us, pops a piece of griddlecake in my mouth.

'Poor wee mite,' she says. 'Poor wee mite.'

Auntie Flora, smiling, cradles me to her. I press my face against her skin, and smell flowers.

So maybe even back then, it was Auntie Flora who hugged me. Mom was always there but not there, shut away from us in a glass box like a princess in a fairytale. And no prince could wake her, not even me.

Thursdays, Auntie Jean took me to the Farmers' Market in Ste Agnès. The people there used strange words for things. I liked to stand by the trestles, listening to the women who bustled round, sniffing pink and gold peaches and picking apples from the towering red mountains. I could work out they said *pommes* when they meant apples, and *pêches* for peaches.

When it was Auntie Jean's turn, I figured she was going to use those funny words too. But she just stood up straight and tall and spoke louder. It seemed to work, kinda.

One of those Thursdays—I must have been about three, I guess—I wandered off and found a stall where they weren't selling fruit and vegetables, or cakes and preserves. This one was laid with thin strips of hide decorated with coloured feathers and patterns of tiny beads, and a sweetish smell of leather hung over it. Those patterns were like nothing I'd ever seen. They had corners and edges and colours that clashed. I stared at them hungrily, wanting to touch.

Someone stirred behind the stall. I looked up and saw two old men with wrinkled faces, their hair black like the night and their skin the colour of strong tea. That was the first time I ever saw faces that looked like mine. I poked out my tongue in surprise, and the old men smiled. Then Auntie Jean caught up with me. Her thin hand took a grip on my arm and she hustled me on.

'Who are those people?' I asked, as she pushed me in front of her out the door.

For a moment, I thought she wasn't going to answer. 'Mohawk,' she said, as if it hurt her jaw to get the words out. 'Injuns.'

My eyes and mouth got big and round. 'Where they from, Auntie Jean?'

'Injun Reserve. Up the road.' Her mouth snapped shut, and I knew it was the end of the conversation.

I saw the Mohawk just one more time before Ed came. Uncle Fraser took me to see the construction site where he worked. He had strong arms that kept me safe and a big, soft smile, and his hair always smelled of Brylcreem. Perched on his shoulders at the foot of a half-built tower, I followed his pointing finger.

'See them up there?' Tiny figures crept along a big steel girder at the top of the tower. 'Them's the spidermen.'

One of them began to lower himself from the girder on a rope, and I figured they must be building a huge steel web.

'You a spiderman too, Uncle Fraser?'

'Nah. Not me. They're Mohawk most of them. Those guys don't seem to mind the heights.'

He must have realized I was trembling, because he lifted me down.

'Hey, big guy. What's the matter? Guess it's time we went and got ourselves some ice-cream, eh?'

If the Mohawk looked like me, I wanted to know, did that make me an Injun? And if so, would I have to be a spiderman too?

Chapter 2

It was Uncle Fraser who brought Ed home that first time. On payday, he and Uncle Donal would bring a few guys back from work for a cookout and a few beers. Then one time, in the summer before I started kindergarten, Ed came with them.

He drove his own pickup and brought a crate of Molson's. He cracked beers with everyone, and laughed and joked. He told Uncle Donal that there was only one way to get the barbecue good and hot, and told Auntie Jean that this was the best goddamn salad dressing he'd tasted in a long while. He flashed his teeth and showed off his paunch and filled the yard with the sound of his voice.

And he talked with Mom.

Mom must have been feeling pretty good that day. She helped with the cooking, and she stood up with Auntie Jean and Auntie Flora serving the salad and the buns. But she sat down again when they started to eat, and now she looked tired.

Ed was the first one lining up for dessert. He walked past the fruit and the angel food cake and the ice cream, and stopped right by a big golden peach pie.

'Which one of you gals made this great looking pie, eh?'

'That would be Margaret,' Auntie Jean answered. 'Sit down, Maggie. I'll deal with this.'

But Ed looked Mom right in the eye, just as if he hadn't heard, and said, 'C'mon, eh? Let the cook cut me a slice of her own pie and I'll see if it doesn't taste as good as it looks.' He leaned towards her. 'Make it a big one, eh?' he said, winking. 'I've a pretty fair appetite.'

Mom blushed. Auntie Jean got stuck with her mouth open. Mom's knife sliced into the piecrust, and the sticky yellow juice oozed up.

After that it was kinda natural that the two of them should sit down together. I could see all the grownups smiling to each other, and whispering.

'Hey, wouldja look at that?'

'I haven't seen Maggie look so good in ages.'

'Well, who'da thought it?'

I bit into the last of my wiener. It had gone cold. Ed didn't look like no prince to me, so why'd Mom wanna wake up for him?

The women went inside to do the dishes, and Ed and Uncle Fraser started to play ball with the older cousins. I crept back under the lilac bush and hunkered down to watch. I could hear shouts of *strike one! strike two!* and the thwack of the ball hitting the bat. Someone missed a catch. The ball rolled near where I was sitting and I crawled out to get it.

When I stood up, clutching the ball in my hands, Ed was standing on the grass in front of me.

My head came up level with his belt buckle. I stared at it because I couldn't see anything else. It was a heavy, shiny maple leaf. Its veins stuck out all over, like it was angry, and I wondered if it was mad at me, or because of having to hold up Ed's pants.

When I looked up, Ed was looking right through me, like he was counting the blades of grass under my feet. I looked down. My feet were still there, okay, but they looked kind of thin. Ed went on staring and counting. The rest of me started to feel like it was fading away. I knew that if he went on counting for long enough, I'd disappear altogether.

My fingers got so thin they couldn't hold the ball. It slid right through them and hit the grass with a thud. Ed looked at it like he'd only just noticed it. Then he scooped it up.

I heard Auntie Jean's voice, calling from the house. Auntie Flora came up behind me and took my hand in hers.

'This is Maggie's son,' she told Ed. 'His name's Terry.'

Ed grinned, and pinched me on the cheek, the way some grownups do when they don't know anything about kids. He could see me all right. But that was right there in front of everyone. I knew he could go ahead and make me invisible again, any time he wanted.

It all happened so fast, Mom and Ed getting married. Everyone assumed they would buy a plot of land by Auntie Jean and Uncle Donal's place, like the other uncles had done. I heard the aunts planning all the things they would do to help make us a new home. It sounded like fun. I'd still be able to run in and out of Auntie Jean's kitchen and eat griddle cakes and bury myself in Auntie Flora's flowery scent. Plus I'd have a whole new bedroom built specially for me. But Ed had other ideas. He took us away to his house the other side of the city, more than an hour's ride away. By the time I started kindergarten, I had a new home, a new father, and a new name.

No one told me that they'd registered me in Ed's name. When the teacher doing roll call said 'Terry Ruskin', I waited for someone else to speak up. She said it again. Then she looked right at me and said, 'Well, Terry Ruskin, I know you're here, because I can see you looking at me.'

I heard someone whisper behind me, 'That native kid's so dumb he doesn't even know his own name.' One kid giggled, then another. I put my hands up to my hot cheeks.

At recess we were bundled outside the classroom into the schoolyard. At one end were some swings and a rusty teeter-totter. I ran towards them with the rest of our class. But before we reached them our way was blocked by a line of bigger kids.

'We gotta rule around here,' said a redheaded girl. 'No little Injuns allowed on the swings.'

I started to say, 'But I'm not ...' Then the line of big kids bent in on itself, and trapped me and three other brown-skinned, dark-haired children. Round and round they swung, chanting:

Eenie, meenie, minie, mo,
Catch an Injun by the toe,
If he hollers, let him go,
Eenie, meenie, minie, mo.

The circle rushed in on us, and pulled one of the boys to the ground. The red-haired girl straddled him and pinched him until he hollered as loud as he could. Then the circle parted and let him go. And it began all over again.

My knees were shaking. I crossed my legs and my hands clutched at my prick. The red-haired girl saw me.

'Look,' she jeered. 'This one's going to pee himself.'

They swept towards me, howling. For a second I was in mid-air, then my back hit the surface of the yard and the girl was kneeling, her legs either side of me, her bum pressing down on my chest.

'I betcha this one's gonna holler good.'

And her thin, mean fingers found the soft flesh on the inside of my arm and pinched hard. I yelled. But not loud enough for her.

I could see a ring of scabby pink knees, tramping up and down, around and around. Around and around and around. Then footsteps came running. The wall of knees wobbled and fell back. Three pairs of legs in long trousers towered over the two of us on the ground.

The girl let go of my arm. Over her shoulder, I saw the faces of the giants who had come to rescue us. They had black hair and dark skin, like mine. And though their hair was cut short and their clothes were like any of the other kids, I recognized them. Like the spidermen, like the stallholders at the Farmers' Market, they were Mohawk.

The Mohawk boys gathered up the other two little kids and turned to leave.

'What about this one?' asked the red-haired girl from her seat on my chest. 'Don't you want him?'

If the Mohawk thought I was an Injun, I thought, maybe they'd keep me safe from the circle of knees and the girl with pinching fingers. But would they take me up with them on that big steel web? Would I have to be a spiderman?

The tallest of the Mohawks shrugged. 'He's not one of ours. You can keep him.'

The red-haired girl looked down at me, puzzled. She shrugged and pinched me again, without much enthusiasm. Then she got up and wandered away, scuffing her shoes as she went.

When I was sure she was gone, I rolled over onto all fours. I had a row of red marks on the inside of my arms that smarted so I couldn't hold my arms to my sides. And I knew by the damp feeling inside my pants that I hadn't managed to hold on.

Ed was in the kitchen when I got home that night. He was cleaning his boots at the table, a copy of the funnies spread out to catch the dirt.

He liked to sit where he had a good view of the room. It drove him crazy if Mom or me walked round behind him. I figured he could see me all right, but most of the time I wished he couldn't. He looked at me the way a bird dog looks at a duck he knows he's not allowed to chase. Biding his time.

'I think it's time you and I came to an understanding, boy,' he said.

He put down the brushes and motioned me to come and stand by him. I didn't want to, but without Mom to hide behind,

I had nowhere else to go. So I stood as far away as I dared.

'I got this problem, eh? See, I'm gonna have to raise you as my son. And I'm not about to let an Injun boy in my house.'

His voice was soft and low, like he was sharing a secret with me.

Injun boy? I wasn't an Injun. Even the Mohawk knew that. So why did people keep telling me I was?

'I got nothing against Injuns, so long as they keep to their Reserves. Hunting, fishing, trapping. Loafing about on government money all day. That's what they want, eh? Well, okay. Just so long as they don't go taking white men's jobs.'

Ed leaned forward till I could feel his breath right in my face. It didn't smell so good.

'Your father, he didn't understand. He came off the reserve, eh? And that's where he went wrong. He wrecked your mom's life, just about. But she's been lucky. Now she's got me. And I'm gonna put things right for her.'

But I didn't have a father, did I? I'd never had a father. It'd always just been me and Mom and the aunts and the uncles.

He poked at my chest and I looked down. His finger was thick and covered in hairs. He scrubbed his hands every day under the tap, but they were always dirty. 'But I've still got you to deal with, boy. You don't belong here and you don't belong on the reserve. So I'm going to do you a favour, boy. I'm going to beat the Injun out of you.'

His voice was so friendly and reasonable I almost didn't take in what he was saying. But something in his eyes scared me bad. Scared me too much to tell Mom what he'd said. But I thought about it a lot. If it was true I had a dad no one ever told me about, and if he was an Injun, a whole lot of things started to make sense.

The next day at recess, I strode across to the far side of the schoolyard where the big kids were playing ball and tugged at the sleeve of the Mohawk boy that had led the rescue.

'You're wrong,' I said. 'I am one of you. My dad's Indian. So there.'

The Mohawk boy started to laugh. The other two from yesterday's raiding party gathered round.

'Oh, yeah? What band is he?' he demanded.

I didn't know what a band was. My courage wanted to curl up in a ball and play dead. But I held myself stiff and looked him in the eye.

'I don't know. No one will tell me about him. But he is Indian. He is.'

The boy looked me up and down.

'Okay,' he said. 'If you're Mohawk, prove it. Mohawk can climb, right?'

'I know about that!' I said. 'I know about spidermen.'

'Everyone knows about spidermen,' he said. 'You see that tree?' He pointed to an old maple by the school wall, its leathery green leaves beginning to yellow. 'You climb that tree, we'll know you're one of us.'

'You mean it? For real?'

The three grinned at each other.

'Yeah. Sure. You climb that tree, and you can join our band.'

I ran for the trunk of the tree. The first part was simple. One branch hung down real low and it made an easy foothold. The next step was harder. It was a longer reach and the bark was smooth. But I made it, and straddled the branch. The three Mohawk were bumming around underneath, tossing a ball between them.

'Go on,' one of them yelled. 'You can do it.'

I reached for the branch over my head and pulled myself up to stand. The trunk had knots and branches all round, but they all seemed to be too high or too far round for me to reach. I hugged the trunk and felt with my foot till I found a ledge, and hauled with my arms. Then it hit me how much space there was between me and the ground

My arms clung to the trunk, one foot balanced on the edge of a knot, the other swinging in mid-air. I couldn't go back and I couldn't go forward, and I was too terrified to yell. Then the bell went for the end of recess, and I heard the three Mohawk laugh.

'So long, little brave,' the biggest one shouted, and they ran off to line up.

I couldn't move. No one saw me. After about a thousand years, I managed to ease myself out along a branch around seven feet up. And that is how they found me, arms and legs wrapped so tight round the branch they had to peel me away. The teacher who came out to look for me when I didn't show up after recess sent me to the principal's office, and I had the backs of my legs whacked six times with a ruler for climbing a tree that was off limits and for missing the recess bell.

But up in that tree I'd figured out why I had a dad who'd never been there. He was waiting for me to be a good enough Indian. Then he'd come back for me.

Chapter 3

For the first few months after Ed and Mom got married, the uncles and aunts mostly kept away. They came once or twice, and I always clung to them and cried when it was time for them to go, and Ed told Mom that she was 'too soft on the boy.' Christmas came, and Auntie Jean asked if we all wanted to go over there for Christmas. I heard Ed on the phone to her.

'Well, now. That's nice of you. But you know how being with a lot of people tires Maggie, eh? And seeing you always seems to upset the boy. I'd sure like to spend Christmas just the three of us, here. Like a proper family. And don't you go spoiling them with a lot of presents now. I can take care of them just fine.'

So we didn't see Auntie Jean and Auntie Flora at Christmas.

Ed assigned us our chores. Mine was to take the garbage out, and to set the table before meals and clear away afterwards, as well as to keep my room tidy and make my own bed. In the fall I had leaves to clear from the yard, and in the winter snow to keep off the paths and the drive. If I failed, Ed would mutter something about 'lazy good-for-nothing Injuns' and I would feel the back of his hand on my ear or across my backside—but never in front of Mom.

Mom's job was to clean and cook and do the laundry. Ed, once a week, took the pickup to the supermarket in the next town, so Mom only needed to buy the few bits and pieces that could be got in the *dépanneur* down the road. And of course he earned the money that kept us all.

'I don't want you doing a lot of socialising,' he told her. 'You've got a home and a family to look after, and you haven't been used to that.' And to me he'd say, 'Don't you go bringing kids home from school to be bothering your mom with, eh?'

So we didn't get to know anyone here, either.

Mom was getting tireder and tireder. By Easter, the little head of steam that had built up in her when she met Ed had worn off, and she was struggling to keep going. Too often when he came home from work, Ed would look round the house and click his tongue and say, 'Now, your sister, Jean: she kept a nice house.' And Mom would battle to keep up Auntie Jean's standards.

One day, Mom didn't get up when I came back from school. I went and stood at the door of the room she shared with Ed. She was lying on the bed, her eyes closed. I knew she was asleep because these days when she was awake she mostly looked like she was waiting for something bad to happen.

Ed was coming home soon, and there was gonna be trouble if the supper wasn't on the table. But I didn't want to wake her. So I figured I'd make supper.

The only thing I knew how to make was peanut butter and jelly sandwiches, but I knew Ed liked those because he had them in his lunch pail sometimes. And these were going to be the best peanut butter and jelly sandwiches that ever were. I was going to make Mom real proud of me.

I got out the bread and cut the slices good and thick, and I didn't cut myself once. I found some butter, and a new jar of peanut butter and some grape jelly that was in the fridge. The butter was hard so it went on lumpy. But the peanut butter was easier. I put plenty of that on. The jelly slopped on top. I put another slice of bread on top and gave it a squeeze to make sure it all stuck. A bluish-purple stain oozed up through the white of the bread and more dripped out of the side. It looked pretty good.

I licked the jelly off my fingers and started on the next one. I worked on, listening all the time for the sound of Ed's pickup in the drive. The wobbly tower of sandwiches in the middle of the table kept growing. I figured this was the finest supper anyone had ever seen, and I wondered if I could be a chef as well as an Indian Brave.

I was kneeling on the table to balance the last sandwich on top of my tower when I heard Mom in the doorway behind me.

'Hey, Mom. Look, I've made supper …' I started to say. Then I saw her dead white face.

I stepped back off the table and looked. I saw a storm of crumbs over the floor. I saw the blobs and splodges and smears of purple and brown splattered across the table like kindergarten finger-paints. And in the middle, I saw a crooked stack of sandwiches bleeding jelly.

Mom didn't say a word. But she moved fast. There was nothing else to eat, and we were all out of time anyhow. She cut my tower of sandwiches as neatly as she could into quarters and arranged them on plates. Between us, we swept the floor and wiped the table and hid the empty jars as best as we could. By the time we heard the rattle of chains and the tires of Ed's big shiny pickup crunching on the snow, the table was set and everything was clean again.

The red second hand on the kitchen clock went round in a full circle. We heard Ed taking off his parka, his boots. Mom and I stood side by side, our arms pressed together and our breath held all tight inside our chests.

Ed came through the door one shoulder at a time and stood looking at the plates on the table.

'What's this?'

Mom took a step forward. 'I'm sorry. I know it's not what you were expecting but there wasn't anything …'

Ed's head turned slowly, a piece of heavy machinery. 'You

know I hate it when people lie to me, eh?'

Mom wiped the back of her hand across her face. A smear of jelly stuck there like a bruise.

'How about you open the icebox?' he said. Mom rubbed her hand on her apron and Ed went red. 'You do know where the icebox is, eh?'

Mom squeezed past, holding herself stiffly, like she was trying not to touch him.

'You wanna tell me what you see?'

'Steak,' she said.

'Steak, eh? Mmm-mm. Well, bring it on out. Put it on the plates.'

Mom looked round to see if he'd gone crazy, but Ed had put on his 'C'mon everyone and join in' act. Moving slowly, like she was in a dream, Mom took the steaks out of their packaging and set them down at the table.

'For what we are about to receive, may the Lord make us truly thankful.' He opened his eyes and smiled broadly. 'Why don't you taste one of these tender, juicy steaks, eh?'

The frost on the meat smoked a little in the heat of the room. Mom pressed her lips closed. The silence was so loud I thought my ears were going to pop. Like she was a puppet and Ed was pulling the strings, Mom picked up the block of frozen red meat and put a corner of it in her mouth.

Ed pushed his chair back and crowed. 'What is wrong with this picture?'

Mom gagged and dropped the meat. She wiped her hand across her mouth.

'Excuse me?' Ed leaned forward. 'I didn't quite catch that.'

'It's still frozen,' she said, her voice so small that Ed's breathing smothered it.

'Well, imagine that! And what do you have to do to frozen steak before you can eat it?'

Mom stared at the table, like she was wishing she was underneath it. 'You thaw it. And you cook it.'

'My, she's a quick study. Only problem is ...' The relentless cheeriness drained out of Ed's voice. 'That requires planning ahead. Something you just can't do.'

Mom tried to stand, but Ed reached across the table and pushed her back down. 'So here's what we're gonna do,' he said. 'I'm gonna decide what we're gonna have for supper each night, and I'm gonna see you take it out of the icebox before I go to work in the mornings.'

Mom's face turned the colour of the frost-covered steaks. 'I can—' she began.

'No. You can't.' He picked up one of the plates of sandwiches and waved it under her nose. 'You can't even make a sandwich right.'

Something pinged inside my head. 'No fair!' I yelled. 'She didn't make these sandwiches. I did. She was asleep and I didn't want to wake her and ...'

Mom's head drooped towards the table. Ed got to his feet.

'Is what the boy says right?'

Mom shook her head, her eyes hidden. 'I'm sorry ... I didn't mean ...'

Ed took hold of her arm and jerked her to her feet.

'I'm working my ass off all day for you and the boy, and you're lying around in bed?'

He put his hand at the side of her face and jerked it round. 'You're lucky to have me, gal.' He flicked his wrist back and I saw her head jolt back as his wedding ring caught her cheek. 'A man like my pa would have kicked you and the boy right out in the snow for that.' Slap. 'You've been spoilt so bad no one else'd give you house room.' Slap.

I didn't know how I was going to move, my legs were shaking so bad. But he was hurting my mom. I staggered across the room, reached up, and swung my full weight from his arm.

I hung a moment, my feet off the ground, while he shook me like a rat. I heard a small, choked sound from Mom and I hit the floor. Ed half dragged, half carried me from the room and dropped me on the bed.

'I'll deal with you later,' he said.

He went out and after a bit I heard a door slam, the other side of the house. I stuck my head under the pillow, but I couldn't shut out the sounds that came from their room.

What felt like hours later, the door opened and it was Ed.

'Listen up,' he said. 'We've each got our chores to do, eh? You gotta learn and your mom's gotta learn. You don't interfere.'

His fingers began undoing his belt. The veins on the silver maple leaf buckle were throbbing. And this time I knew for sure. It was mad at me.

The belt came out of his pants and slid through his hands like a long black snake.

'Take your pants down, boy.'

My hands were shaking too much to manage the button and I had to drag my pants down over my hips, pulling my underpants to half-mast.

'I told you I'd beat the Injun out of you,' he murmured. 'And I'll do it, boy. I'll do it.'

The first blow hit me across the buttocks and knocked me face down onto the bed. I tried to scream, and my mouth filled with blanket. I heard Ed grunt, and the next blow hit my thighs. I began to sob, too hurt to make much noise. The sound of the belt hitting my skin made my ears ring, and I couldn't understand why my mom didn't hear it and come and stop the hurt.

I must have been tiring him. The grunts got louder, the blows got slower. At some point they stopped. For a long time I didn't dare move. I heard the screen door creak and bang, and the pickup backing down the drive. Then my mom came.

She covered me over with a blanket and sat by the side of the bed, stroking my hair. When I could bear to move, I rolled over on my side and looked up into her face. A darkening bruise spread across one side and she was cradling one arm in the other.

'Call Auntie Jean,' I pleaded. 'Make them come and take us away.'

Mom shook her head dully.

'We can't do that, sweetie. He's my husband. We have to stay here now.'

'Please, Mom.' I tugged at the front of her dress. 'Before he comes back.'

She took my hands in hers. They were cold. 'It'll be okay,' she promised. 'You'll see. We'll be good. We won't upset Ed any more.'

PART II

1971

Chapter 4

It had gotten dark by the time I started out on the five-mile trek to the house. The school bus from the Sec left over an hour ago, but lately I hadn't bothered a whole lot with school. Not since that time around my thirteenth birthday when Mom got so sick that even Ed couldn't ignore it. When he finally drove her to the hospital and the doctors said there was nothing they could do and sent her home again.

The copies of the *Gazette* in the box on the corner were full of tonight's hockey game between the Canadiens and the Leafs. A cakewalk, they said. All the Habs had to do was leap over the boards and the Leafs were goners for sure. I felt in my pocket for a quarter, but all I found was a nickel, a piece of string and a chewing gum wrapper. I shrugged and kept going.

There had been a thaw. Dead brown scabs of grass poked through the snow in the front yards of the houses I passed. Slick grey slush covered the sidewalks and seeped through the canvas tops of my running shoes. Two miles. Three. A car went by, spraying a fountain of muddy water from its wheels. The cold soaked through my pant leg and eight years of bruising and scars woke up and began to throb.

Ed's rusted pickup slumped on the drive, one tire flat. The screen door creaked and slammed behind me. I kicked off my wet runners and socks, and padded bare-foot through the kitchen. The floor had a tacky feel and something on the table had started to smell.

I stopped at the door of their bedroom. My mother lay on the bed—a little bundle of bones messing the sheets. Her sunlight-coloured hair had faded till it was no kind of colour at all, and in the light of the bare bulb over the bed, you could see the lines of her skull.

I went and sat by the bed. *Why didn't you leave while there was still time?* I pleaded with her, like every night since she came down sick. *Why did you have to wait till it was too late?*

The corner of her mouth was wet with spittle and I wiped it away. I tried to hold her hand, but it twitched and fluttered in mine like a bird that's hurt. So I moistened her lips a little with a sponge, like the nurse had taught me, and smoothed the sheets as best as I could.

The pain must have gotten worse, because she started to moan and tug at the blankets. Ed appeared in the doorway, a syringe and a phial of morphine in his hand. He jerked his thumb over his shoulder, and I got up and slipped out, pressing myself against the doorjamb so I didn't have to touch him.

When I looked back he was holding her arm, feeding the needle into the wasted muscle. One of the guys I'd started hanging round with at the mall told me morphine was the same thing as heroin, and how much I could get for it on the street. I knew where Ed kept it. I could have taken it easy. But I'd never do that to her.

I went and lay down in my room. I didn't exactly sleep. Most nights I lay listening for the sound of my mother's groans, Ed's shuffling feet.

After a while I rolled onto my stomach and felt under the mattress for my tin of charcoal pencils and some sheets of scrap art paper. I didn't turn on the main light. It was safer not to attract attention. Making do with the old bed-light, I pulled my knees up at the right angle for a makeshift drawing table, and started to draw. Drawing made a safe place inside my head. Things got so they were at arm's reach, not pressed right up against my skull. But it was like Mom's morphine. You always had to have another shot.

I drew Mom's face, just as it was, lying on the bed in the room next door. Trying to remember every line. Concentrating on getting the right sort of hatching to bring out the hollows in her cheeks and the floppy wetness at the corners of her mouth. It was hard to make changes in the charcoal marks, but I'd learnt a trick. I'd keep back a piece of bread from my lunch pail and knead it to a ball in my hands. It lifted some of the charcoal, softening lines, making highlights. When the sketch was done, I added it to the pile of drawings under the mattress.

Sometime after midnight, I heard snores coming from the living room. I got up again and went in. The television was on, the sound turned right down. The Habs were beating the Leafs 3-1 again in replay. I watched Richard feed a long lead pass to Beliveau, and Beliveau slide the puck under the goaltender's elbow. *He shoots! He scores!*

Ed was slumped on the chesterfield, his mouth open. The flickering black and white light turned his face grey, like he was a sketch too. He looked puny—except for his gut, which oozed over the top of the maple leaf buckle.

I felt in the lining of my pocket where I'd hidden the knife. *Soon.* I thought. *Not yet. You're not going to miss one day of Mom's suffering.*

The week before she died, the morphine quit working. Mom's faint cries filled the house like cobwebs. I stopped going out. For five days we were locked together, Ed, Mom and me, wrestling with her pain. Then, at four minutes past six one grey, wet, miserable morning, the noise stopped. Mom was free.

As soon as they let me, I went in to see her. She was lying

on the bed, just as she'd lain for the past six weeks. Her face was yellow, like someone had made a model of her in wax. Only they hadn't been too particular about the truth. The wax model looked a whole lot younger than Mom had done—like the last eight years had never happened.

I thought about Ed, and I felt in my pocket for the knife, to make sure it was still there. The blade was so sharp against my thumb it gave me a hard-on.

I had it all figured out, what I was going to do. I'd wait till the night after the funeral, when Ed was asleep. He was carrying a lot of fat, but it was a long knife. It'd reach his heart. Then when he was dying, I'd slide the knife out and take his fucken scalp, so they'd know it was an Indian that killed him. I hoped he'd still be alive, so he'd know what I was doing. So he'd know that in eight years he'd never beaten the Indian out of me.

After I'd watched him bleed to death, I'd take the knife and the scalp, and go back to my den. To the safe place where I'd hidden when I was just a kid. When I was still dumb enough to believe my real dad was going to come and take us away from Ed. No one was gonna find me in that den. And the thing about dying of exposure is that you just sort of drift off to sleep. I'd read about that too. It sounded good.

The ground was beginning to thaw; so we didn't have long to wait for the funeral. That day in church, I kept my hand on the knife the whole time. Some old biddy with her hair scragged up in a bun told me to take my hands out of my pockets, but I snarled at her, pulling back my lips to show her my teeth. She went all pale and turned away, and after that she left me alone.

I didn't take a whole lot of notice of what was going on, because I kept thinking all the time about sticking the knife into Ed's chest and watching the blood pumping out of him. Washing everything clean with Ed's blood. I didn't see the car waiting outside the cemetery gates, or the two people standing on the sidewalk, until our pathetic little procession trailed out and a woman stepped forward and put her hand on my arm.

'Terry? My name's Shirley. I'm from the Children's Aid Society, and I've come to take you to a place of safety.'

I stared at her, not taking in what she was saying. I just knew she was getting in my way. I glimpsed Ed's face over her shoulder, saw my revenge slipping out of my hands, and I lunged after him, a scream burning my throat. The man by the gates grabbed my arms. Other faces turned, startled, frightened. Ed jerked round and started to hurry away.

'Don't lose him,' someone said, and I thought they meant me. Then a cop car pulled up alongside Ed and two policemen stepped out, blocking his path.

I went on screaming and struggling until their groping hands found the hard edge of the knife in my pocket. I saw it lifted out and passed on, hand over hand, till a cop took it and I knew I'd lost. Then I went limp.

Chapter 5

A room somewhere. A little cot-bed with a sheet and a blanket. The Hunter sat on the bed. The wall in front of him was grey. That was all he saw. A grey wall. They had taken away his pictures, and his head was empty. Nowhere safe to go.

Without the hunt, the Hunter had no purpose.

A key grated in the lock. Voices.

'You know our first choice would always be that he is looked after by someone from the family.' That was the Welfare woman. She came every day.

'He's been like this ever since the funeral? He hasn't spoken?' New voice. Different.

'It's called dissociation. An extreme response to trauma.'

'Has he eaten?'

'Not a lot. He'll let us spoon feed him a bit. That's all.' A pause, then, 'Why don't you speak with him?'

A face came and placed itself in front of the Hunter. A woman with faded red hair. *She was at the funeral*, he realized. *She looks like ...*

No. Don't think about that.

'Terry? Do you remember me, sweetie?'

Something dredged itself up from where ... Ed ... had buried it. A smell of flowers. There were flowers at the funeral. ... Ed ... had brought a wreath. Big white flowers with a heavy, dead scent.

'I used to come and see you when you were tiny. When you lived with Auntie Jean.'

No flowers at the den. After the crows and the jays had picked his bones clean. Just maple saplings. Birch. They'd grow well. The soil would be good, afterwards. Maybe a tree would grow through his bones.

For a flickering second he could *see* a tree. Then his mind snapped shut and there was the grey wall. And between him and the wall a face. It bobbed up and down like a balloon.

Soft. Something soft and comforting.

Flora.

The Hunter's lips moved, but no sound came out.

'You've got some more cousins now, Terry. One of them is just starting school.'

The trapdoor in his mind opened a chink, and before it shut again the Hunter floated above the schoolyard, hearing the recess bell and a sound of laughter.

'They want me to ask you if you'd like to come and live with us, sweetie. With me and Uncle Fraser.'

The Hunter tried to focus. The pink balloon face floated in front of him. And something else. Long. Lifting up. *An arm.* Arms hit. That's what they do. Arms hurt.

Get down. Protect the bits that hurt most. Try not to make too much noise. Stay still till it's all over.

There was a noise behind him—air let out of a balloon. Someone scrambling to their feet.

'Dear God.'

'I'm sorry.' The welfare woman's voice. 'I guess I should have said. He doesn't let anyone touch him.'

'What did that bastard *do* to him?'

'We don't know the details, but the signs are that he's been terribly abused. He has some healed fractures.

Deep tissue bruising. And his behaviour—'

The woman the Hunter once knew was angry. 'Couldn't you people have stopped this?'

A shuffle of papers.

'The family kept themselves to themselves. And the boy was in school, mostly. Abusers can be very crafty about hiding what they do. No one suspected anything until the nurse spotted signs of his mother's injuries ...'

The face came back again. A hand hovered over the Hunter's head, and he whimpered.

'I'm sorry,' the face said. 'I can't. I wish I could, but I can't. I have to put my own kids first.' The silence went on so long the Hunter began to think she had gone. Then he heard her voice again. She spoke quickly, the pitch rising. 'He was such a sweet little boy, you know.'

The Hunter heard her footsteps hurrying down the corridor. The link to a life before there was a Hunter, when there was a boy in a garden ...

'I'm a man on the land, I'm a selkie on the sea ...'

'Terry? Did you say something?'

He had thought the welfare woman was gone too. No more sound came from him, and after a while she closed the door, and locked it.

Chapter 6

We were in the car for a long time. Me and the welfare woman. Days, maybe. Sometimes the Hunter took over and I lost track, but I was mostly living in my own skin again. We stopped several times at a diner, got out, peed, ate and drank a little. The weather changed from wet to cold and clear. The car moved fast under a blue sky scarred with high white clouds. After a time, it slowed and started to snake around. My ears hurt. Late afternoon, a long time after we passed the last town, the car stopped.

The welfare woman opened the door and helped me out. I stood by the car and looked at my running shoes. She took my arm and I walked alongside her, still looking at my runners. The asphalt underfoot turned into cedar chippings. The paths sloped down a ways and turned a corner.

The air here smelled different than back home. On one side it was crackling dry, but on the other I could feel moisture on my cheek. I turned my head, lifted my nose a little, sniffed like an Indian tracker, and stopped.

The welfare woman stumbled. Then she stopped, too, and gawked at me.

A long low rail ran beside the path. I held on to it, my eyes closed, letting my other senses open up. I could feel the wind in my face. I could smell pine resin. I opened my mouth and drank in great gulps of it. Then I opened my eyes.

I was at one end of a narrow lake. The other end disappeared off into tomorrow. Below where I stood, the wind ruffled the edges of the water, but out there it could have been polished stone. A stone so blue you could lose yourself in the colour. At either side—like bold strokes of a palette knife from the sky to the lake—were mountains. Green-black pine over an ash-grey beach, peaks of dazzling white snow …

No. The snow wasn't just white. In the sunshine it was a hundred different colours. Pink. Blue. Gold. You only saw white if you were too lazy to look.

The welfare woman tugged at my arm. I paid no heed. In my mind, I had my sketchbook in my hand, pencils, crayons.

The Hunter's still here, inside me, biding his time. And the quarry's still out there, somewhere. Alive.

She tugged again and I jerked my arm free. Another set of footsteps crunched on the cedar chips. The welfare woman gave a groan of relief and moved away up the path.

'Kate. How are you?' She was flustered. I flustered her. 'I'm sure glad you could take this boy on. I don't know where else we could have tried.'

'Don't fret,' said the other one. 'You did the right thing.'

'It's not easy from the other side of the country, you know. But after his aunt …'

She looked at me and shut her mouth. The two of them moved away and I heard them whispering their grown-up secrets. Odd words drifted back to me. The welfare woman's mostly. 'Terribly withdrawn … Hasn't really spoken since … The way he reacted … You couldn't blame her …' Then footsteps on their way back down the path. Not the welfare woman. She wore those high heels that slipped and tripped her when she hurried. This new one had flat, soft-soled shoes. She planted her feet firmly, like someone used to walking on grass.

She stood beside me by the rail. I waited for her to take charge, start giving me orders. But she stayed quiet, and I kept looking at the lake until I forgot about her.

The sun dipped behind the shoulder of the mountain and the water deepened from blue to violet. Out on the lake, something howled—one long, sad note. I shivered and pulled back from the rail.

'It's the loons,' said a voice at my elbow. An arm reached out, a forefinger pointing. Two small dark shapes were moving, low down in the water. Long-necked birds. 'The first time you hear them, they sound so lonely, it'd break your heart. But that's their chat. When the humans are off the lake and they've got it to themselves again.'

I turned and saw the top of her head. She'd have to stand on tiptoe to reach my chin. Her head was thrown back, and in the gathering shadows her eyes held steady on my face. She made me think of one of the little brown mice that came out at dusk, watching me in my den as if they had no call to be scared of a human boy.

She smiled when I looked down, and held out her hand. 'Hello. I'm Kate Howgill. And I suppose you must be Terry Ruskin?'

Her voice was kind of weird. Her 't's popped off her tongue, and her 'r's were like the whirr of a tiny motor. She said … his … name and something twisted inside me.

'Not Ruskin.' I hadn't tried my voice in a long time and it had rusted up tight. I spat words. 'I'm Terry Havelock.'

The welfare woman gave a muffled squeal of protest, but the mouse woman didn't flinch.

'Of course. I'm sorry. Ruskin was your stepfather's name, wasn't it? We don't need to use it ever again.' She waited for me to give a nod in acknowledgement then held out her hand. 'So will you come with me, Terry Havelock?' She saw my eyes still glued to the lake and misunderstood. 'Don't fret. You can still see the lake where we're going.'

I didn't trust her, exactly. But I didn't have a whole lot of choice.

I woke up slowly the next day, feeling the smooth, clean sheets and something light and squashy covering me up. Good smells were worming their way under the door. Bacon. And maple syrup.

I figured the door would be locked, like it had been in the place they took me after the funeral. But it opened when I pressed the handle. I could hear the *pop pop* of bacon frying, and the sizzle of pancake batter being ladled onto a griddle. *Oh jeez: real maple syrup.* In spite of myself, my mouth was watering, and my stomach gurgled loudly. *Don't let them get to you.*

The mouse woman's head appeared at the end of the corridor, her hair pushed back out of her eyes, her face all pink from the heat of the stove.

'There's time for a shower if you'd like one,' she said. 'Second door on the left. Don't be too long. Breakfast is ready.'

The head disappeared again. I went into the bathroom and stood with my eyes closed under a torrent of hot water. A rap on the door, and the mouse woman said, 'Come on. Don't let it get cold.' I went into the kitchen.

A stack of just-brown pancakes steamed on a plate, next to a jug of warm maple syrup. The bacon was curled on another plate, its fat crisp, the pink meat peppered with black where the sugar-cure had toasted on its surface.

The mouse woman was helping herself, delicately putting a pancake and a piece of bacon onto the plate in front of her. The chair back reached the top of her head.

'Hungry?'

The Hunter doesn't eat. Not to enjoy it. Eating's just what you do to stay alive, for as long as you need to stay alive. But I was drooling. My stomach felt like it was trying to climb out through my chest and get to the bacon itself. I sat down slowly, trying to stay in control.

The mouse woman put two pancakes and a slice of bacon onto my plate and, when I didn't say no, poured a little maple syrup over the top. The whole lot vanished, and my stomach quit doing karate chops inside me. I went on staring at my plate. She put four more pancakes and two more slices of bacon on my plate, and this time I covered them all over with as much maple syrup as I dared. The mouse woman didn't say a word.

There were still a bunch of pancakes and bacon left. The mouse woman stopped eating and sat sipping her coffee. She looked at me sidelong so I wouldn't think she was watching me.

I kept eating, making each mouthful last. If I could make it last forever, maybe I could forget about the hunt. The soft, fluffy pancakes soaked up the syrup. I held one in my mouth and squeezed, and maple syrup oozed out over my tongue, liquid and sweet. The bacon crunched and tickled, and left a salt-sweet tang in my mouth after I'd swallowed it.

All gone. I licked syrup and bacon-salt from my lips, and waited for the mouse woman to make her move. But she didn't seem in any hurry to talk. She sat still, cradling her coffee mug in her hands and looking at me.

When I got pissed off with trying to outstare her, I pushed back the chair and made for the window. The sky had greyed up overnight and the wind was stronger. Like she'd said, you could see the lake from here. Today it was slate, with purple shadows where the wind roughed up the water.

I had to get the Hunter back to the hunt.

When I looked back over my shoulder, the mouse woman hadn't turned round. Her back sprang straight up from the base of the chair without quite touching it, like she was used to stretching up to see over things.

'Where am I?' I asked.

She swung round in the chair. 'In a place called Achmore, on the edge of the Rockies.'

'The Rockies? No way.' *Shit. They couldn't have brought me that far.* 'I was in Montreal.'

'You were driven a long way. Do you remember that?'

I shook my head angrily. Something I'd heard at school goosed the back of my mind. The Canadian Pacific Railway, linking Canada together, east to west. Maybe I could use that to get back to Ed. To my revenge.

'The railway. How do you get to there from here?'

'The railway?'

'Yeah. You know. The Canadian Pacific. That runs through the Rockies, doesn't it?'

Her tongue touched her lips. 'The CPR's about a hundred miles south of here,' she said.

Had I made her suspicious? Gotta be careful. Mustn't let her see what the Hunter wants. I shrugged like I couldn't care less and moved away from the window. For something to do, I made a circuit of the room, pacing out my new cell.

'Better class of pokey than the last one I was in,' I said, real casual.

'You're not in prison, Terry. There are no locks on the door.'

'No?' I made a big show of looking around. 'What do you use? Electric fencing?'

Something about the way she looked at me made me feel that was kind of a shitty thing to say. I threw myself into a chair as far away from her as I could get. A pile of newspapers lay on the table in front of me.

The Habs. Jeez. I didn't know what the date was, whether we were still in the Stanley Cup.

I peeled my tongue off the roof of my mouth. 'You got the sports pages?'

'Help yourself.'

I squatted by the table, turning the pages of the paper. This wasn't exactly the *Gazette.* The Habs weren't on the front page. But they were there. Leading the East Division play-offs. I leaned back on my heels and closed my eyes. '*Last night's game a shutout … A crowd of 14,543 … On their feet … Beliveau! Beliveau!*'

'Good news?' the mouse woman asked, from nearby. I opened my eyes, and saw her sitting on one of the low chairs by the table. She sure moved quietly.

'Not bad,' I admitted.

She was in a hurry to get to the point now. She pressed her fingers together in front of her.

'Terry, do you understand why you've been brought here?'

She was going to tell me anyway. Grown-ups always did.

'The child welfare people in Montreal decided it wasn't safe for you to go on living at home. When that happens the first thing they do is to try and trace your family, your parents. Terry, did you know that—'

'Not so hard to try and trace my parents. They're both in the cemetery. I suppose you might have a bit of trouble finding my dad's grave, seeing how no one seems too sure who he was, even.'

'Terry—'

'Anyway, why is it not safe?'

'Pardon?' The mouse woman opened her mouth and shut it again.

'Why is it not safe for me to live there now, when it was safe before?'

'Was it safe before?' Her eyes met mine. Her sharp teeth were nibbling at my defences. 'Terry, we know it wasn't safe, for you or your mother. The people who should have looked after your interests made a terrible mistake not realising it sooner. But that's why you're here. So we can try and put things right.'

'I can put it right.' *The Hunter can put it right.*

'Not by yourself.' She pushed her hair back behind her ears. 'Terry, there are wounds that need to heal.'

She was getting way too forward. *The Hunter stirred, hackles rising.*

'Hey! I'm fit. I haven't had a broken bone for months.'

'There'll be other wounds. Ones you can't see.'

I shrugged. 'Last doctor I saw said no internal bleeding either.'

She had a way of touching the place between her eyes—just lightly, with her finger—when I said something she didn't like.

'Terry, I can help you, but you have to trust me a little—give me something to work with.'

We heard a sound like a bunch of car horns honking and we turned together. A V of geese flew over the lake, wheeled and landed on its slate surface. I counted thirteen Canada geese. Black necks and brown bodies.

'How long was your mother ill, Terry?'

She caught me off guard. I had to screw down doors in my mind to stop pictures of Mom getting out.

'My mother was always sick.'

'You don't remember a time before your mother had cancer?' Her eyes searched my face.

Stupid. You don't know. 'Long time ago before ...' *Before there was a Hunter. Mustn't say that.* 'Long time ago, the aunts took care of her. She was sick then. Not cancer. Sick in the head, kinda. But the aunts went away and there was just her and me and ...' *And ... Ed ... There was Ed. Always Ed.* 'She got sicker. And I couldn't help her.' *So now there was the Hunter. The Hunter had to put things right.*

'Terry, you were a little child when Ed came into your lives. You couldn't help what was happening to your mother. None of it was your fault.'

I pushed back in the chair and stared up at the sky. The leaden grey sky. Closing in, pressing down on the mountains.

'Mom used to say we weren't good enough. If we just tried harder, we could make him stop.'

'She was kidding herself.'

'I know.'

The grey cloud twisted. *If I knew that, why didn't she? Why did she go on saying it would be okay?*

The mouse woman leaned forward, like she'd made up her mind about something. Her little brown face was watching me intently. The hair she'd tucked behind her ears had escaped, and it fell forward against her cheek in a long comma.

'Terry, I'm going to make you a promise.' She held out her hands towards me, palm upwards. 'This is a place people come when they've been terribly hurt. Some adults. Some children. A kind of therapeutic community. And it's your place of safety. For as long as you want it, for as long as you need it—you're home is here with me.'

She was so dumb.

'Until I make too much trouble. Or you get another job.'

'That's not what I said.'

She sat so still. People fidget when they lie, don't they? *Why would she make a promise like that?* the Hunter whined. *A stranger like her?*

She'd have to be a madwoman. Or a saint, which was the same difference.

'Why should I believe you?' I demanded.

'Because this isn't just a job for me. It's part of what I am. You don't walk away from what you are. There's too high a price.'

Chapter 7

For days after that, I kept checking to see if she was going to start shaking beads over me, or chanting or something. But if she was crazy, she was playing it pretty close to her chest.

Another time she said, 'Tell me about Terry Havelock.'

'You got a file, haven't you?'

'I have a file on Terry Ruskin.'

'Same difference.'

'Is it? You didn't seem to think so the other day.'

I was prowling round the room. I passed a mirror and caught sight of myself. The hair on my head was starting to grow out. I ran my hand over my skull and felt it, short and springy like rabbit fur.

'How long is it since my mom's funeral?' I asked.

'Just over two months.'

I ran my hand over my head again.

'It's so long.'

'Long?'

I turned my head from side to side, trying to get used to the look of it.

'He used to shave it. Every Friday night. Last time was the night before the funeral.'

'Why? Why would he do that?'

'He said, "Them lice, eh, they love that dirty black Injun hair."'

I could hear my voice starting to sound like Ed's. It scared me, like I could turn into Ed if I thought about him too much. 'So he got rid of it,' I went on, careful to sound like me. 'Burnt it. But I reckon it made me look like an Indian warrior.'

The mouse woman, Kate, scrunched her eyebrows together a little.

'Some Indian tribes only cut their hair when someone close to them dies,' she said.

We were dying all the time, I thought. Ed just went on killing us a little bit every day. I moved back to the spot by the window where I liked to stand. The sun was shining on the path outside. Up in the mountains the sky was black. Now and again lightning shattered over the peaks, too far away for the thunder to be heard.

'Why did you want to look like a warrior?' Kate asked, from behind me.

'To be like my father,' I said without thinking. 'To make him proud.'

Jeez. Kate baits a hook and I swallow it.

'Do you remember your father, Terry?'

No memories. A picture in my head. 'My father is dead,' I said.

'How do you know that?'

One shoulder twitched, warding something off.

'He's gotta be dead. Else he'd have come back for us.'

A flame of anger seared up inside me, white hot, bright as a blowtorch.

If he's not dead, he's as good as dead. 'Cos if he's not dead, I'm gonna kill him. 'Cos he never came. 'Cos he let Ed do what he did.

'Better he's dead.'

The room was full of paper, pens, crayons, paint. I had lost my temper, kicked a flowerpot through a window, knocked Kate against a table. She'd put me in here to cool off.

A maple leaf, let out from under the melting snow, flapped along the path outside. It caught against the window and clung there, its veins picked out in the bright spring sunshine.

I picked up a sheet of paper and started to draw. In pencil first, then crayon. Trying to capture what I saw. Drawings of leaves started to litter the floor, as if fall had come after winter. But they weren't any of them right.

I found black paper, chalk, white pastille, and some other colours. I started to draw without looking, drawing what was in my head, coming closer and closer. I blended each colour of pastille separately to give it a shine, put shadows under each of the veins …

There. On the paper.

The maple leaf.

I couldn't touch it. Couldn't look away. Couldn't move away.

Kate came in and sat down cross-legged, facing me across the sheet of black paper.

'These are quite something,' she said.

She reached towards the black paper and I flinched. She saw that, and set her hands back in her lap where I could see them.

'A leaf,' she said. 'A maple leaf, in the frost?'

I stared at the floor. I shook my head.

'Not in the frost?'

'… not a leaf …' I croaked.

Kate's voice dropped. 'What is it, Terry?'

It tried to fill my head up with the cold, flat, hard linoleum under my bum. But the scars on my back wouldn't let me rest.

'… 's a belt buckle …'

Her eyebrows screwed up. 'Whose belt buckle, Terry?'

I heard a noise like a whipped puppy, and it was me. I was shaking my head back and forth, as if I could shake off the memories.

'It's okay. You don't have to tell me anything.'

Can't tell. Need to tell. My hands crept towards hers. She saw, and reached out her hands. As soon as they were near enough I grabbed hold and held on.

'Whose buckle is it?' she repeated gently.

'… Ed …' It started as a mumble and grew like a drum beat. 'Ed. ED. **ED. ED.**'

'It's okay. It's okay. Ssshhh.'

Kate unlaced her hands from mine, one finger at a time. She wrapped her arms around me, and held on tight. I was shaking.

'Hush. Hush. Don't fret. You're safe. No one's going to hurt you.'

Someone touching. Touching me. One hand in the small of my back. Another on my shoulder. Pressing lightly. Arms encircling me. My face in her shoulder. Breasts moving, up and down. Warm air on my face, keeping time.

'Tell me,' she whispered into my hair. 'Tell me what he did with the buckle.'

'Hit. He hit the boy.' My body convulsed, memories heaving, retching inside me. 'The boy watched. Watched him undo it. Always made him watch. Used to hit him with the belt. But it wasn't enough. Couldn't beat the Injun out of him. So he hit him with the buckle. With the buckle. With the maple leaf buckle.' I strained against her. 'Oh, jeez. I want it to stop. I want it to stop.'

'It has stopped. It's over. He can't hurt you.'

'The Hunter. The Hunter will finish it.'

Oh, jeez.

The words lay quivering. No taking them back. Kate had heard them, loud and clear.

She loosed her arms and sat up, her eyebrows knotting up.

'Who is the hunter, Terry?' she asked.

'The Hunter will finish it,' I repeated.

Her hands were still touching me, on my shoulder, on my arm. I knew she could feel me trembling.

'How? How will he finish it?'

'Kill. Ed.'

My tongue seemed to fill up my whole mouth. I gagged. Kate's hands slid down my arms, took my hands, turned them palm upwards.

'Is that what the knife was for, Terry? For killing?'

I started to rock back and forth on my haunches. My throat was making a single flat note. *Scared. I'm scared.*

Kate's thumbs rubbed across my palms.

'And what will that do to you, if you kill him?'

Roots through my bones. Tree growing towards the sky.

'Set. The boy. Free.'

'Killing won't set you free.' Her hands tightened their grip on mine, and she shook them. 'If you kill Ed, he'll be a part of you for the rest of your life. You'll never be free of him.'

When the bough breaks the baby will …die.

'Not free to live. Free to die.'

Kate's eyes darkened, her pupils wide open. She looked down at my hands in hers and her hair fell across her face. Then she straightened again.

'Is that what you want, Terry? Is that really what you want?'

Pictures crowded in my head. Mom lying on the bed—a little bundle of bones messing up the sheets. The dream image of Ed, bleeding to death from a hole in his chest while the Hunter scalped him. His blood washing it all clean. The mountains outside. The lake disappearing off into tomorrow. Tomorrow …

Kate pushed a strand of hair back behind her ear. Sunlight caught the side of her face. I could see a pink-red mark on the side of her face, spreading out from a purple line where her cheekbone had hit the side of the table.

I reached out my free hand and touched it with my forefinger.

'I did that.'

'Yes.'

'Does it hurt?'

'Yes, rather.'

She took my hand in hers and held it for a moment against her cheek.

'I'm. Sorry.'

'I know.'

Chapter 8

Summertime. The Habs had won the Stanley Cup and big Jean Beliveau had retired. One chapter closed and another one opening.

Kate had taken me out in a canoe on the lake. My arms moved down and back, the paddle dipped in and out of the water, and the canoe slid forward. The island came closer. If I screwed up my eyes, I could turn the orange bulk of the life jacket in front of me into a pair of broad shoulders. My father's. It's what I used to dream about, in my den, my safe place. I'd dream I was sitting with my father in a canoe, paddling across a lake somewhere.

It was a fibreglass canoe, not birch bark. But you couldn't have everything.

Kate said the Indians believed that the dead didn't go away. The ancestor spirits lived all around us in trees and birds and animals and stuff. I kind of liked the idea that Dad might be watching me.

My shoulders were aching. They weren't used to this yet. I kept my eye on the crease in Kate's shirt, trying to keep time. Away to our right, a pair of loons skimmed over the water, the white necklace on their throats reflected perfectly, upside-down in the glassy green water. As we went by, one of the loons chuckled and they turned away, their wings rattling. A few strokes later I heard them again—a rising pitch, repeated. *What are you doing here? What are you doing here?* The two loons swam past, their necks low over the water.

I looked up and saw the eagle over the tops of the trees, riding the thermals. The loons had seen it coming and were warning it off. The eagle began to spiral upwards, its wings barely moving. I watched it reach its height and hold its position over the canoe.

I was watching it. And it was watching me.

Dad. Watching me.

Don't be a jerk.

Well, it could be, couldn't it?

I felt as if the veins in my throat were all knotted up.

'Oy!' Kate protested. She thrust her paddle out to steady us. Those skinny arms were stronger than they looked: we held. 'What are you doing back there? You'll have us over.'

'Sorry.'

I glanced up once more. The eagle was still hovering over us.

Kate turned the canoe and we paddled round to the far side of the island, making for a little bay with a gently shelving beach. I could hear the *dip, dip* of the paddles, the soft rushing sound of the water under the forefoot. A few minutes later we pulled the canoe well up on the shingle, took off our life jackets and stowed them under the thwarts.

I pulled out my drawing things and climbed a flat rock a little way along the beach. The drop down onto the shingle kind of scared me. But up here you could pretend this was still Indian country. Nothing here but you, the forest and the lake.

Kate let me raid the Art Room for anything I wanted, so I'd tried just about every way I could think of to draw what I saw. Washes of watercolour paint over pen. Layers of pastel, glimmering and translucent. Acrylics. Gouache. I ran the Art Room out of greens and blues and then started on the yellows. I knew I did my best drawing up here.

Kate called me down for lunch. I scrambled down from the rock and she pulled the picnic hamper out from under the thwarts.

'Tell me a story,' I said, wolfing down sandwiches.

'What sort of a story?' she asked.

The eagle was still up there. I could feel it, watching me.

'An Indian story.' I scuffed my feet on the shingle, pretending like I was pulling an idea out of nowhere. 'Y'know any stories about eagles?'

Kate was sitting tucked up like she didn't want to make the beach look untidy. Instead of starting to tell a story, she tilted her head on one side and studied me, the space between her eyebrows all scrunched up.

'What does it mean to you, to be an Indian?'

I chewed on my peanut butter sandwich, feeling for the crunchy bits of peanut in my teeth. It wasn't like you could put Kate off with a smart-ass reply. She'd keep coming at you from different angles until she caught you saying something that mattered.

'It's what made me different,' I said. 'From Ed. From everyone.'

'What about from the Mohawk boys at school?'

My bum cheeks tightened. For a zillionth time, I was hanging from that tree branch, watching the Mohawk boys run away laughing.

'Told you about that already.'

'I know.'

She waited while I hurled a bit of shingle into the water. The stone here was so dark you kept thinking it was going to come off on your fingers. I dragged a piece of it across a page of my sketchbook, but it didn't make a mark.

'You're like some fucken dentist, you know. Poking and probing all the time.'

I saw the corner of Kate's mouth trying not to smile. Her hand was resting up against mine. I could feel the knuckle of her little finger.

'So do I take away the toothache?'

I kicked a pile of pebbles down the beach.

'Maybe.'

'Then stop your blethering and let me probe.'

We both giggled together. *Jeez, she was tricky.* I closed my eyes and forced myself to look down from that branch in the schoolyard.

'I was something else,' I said. 'Something different. Neither one thing or another.'

Kate took a long breath. 'And how does that make you feel?' Her voice was so quiet I had to strain to hear her.

'Dunno.' It was still a long way down. But it felt good too—all the way up there in that place that was mine alone. 'Scared,' I said. 'Special, kinda. Lonely.'

Kate's hand shifted sideways over mine. The palm was warm and callused. She let the silence settle between us. Somewhere out on the water I heard the loon again, warning off the eagle.

'Where do you think you belong?' she asked.

'Nowhere. I don't belong anywhere.'

Kate looked at me sideways, her cheek resting on her knee. 'How about with your father?'

My head scythed round. *If she's jerking me around …* 'You mean like dead?' I jeered.

'No,' she said. She wrinkled up her nose. 'I don't mean *like dead.*'

The hard stones of the beach were digging holes in my bum. I got onto my haunches.

'He didn't exactly belong with us, did he?' I muttered.

'Perhaps he just didn't belong with your mother's family.'

The sun off the lake was smarting my eyes. I squeezed them shut.

'What's the difference? He's dead, anyway.'

'Is he?'

Kate's hand came to rest in the middle of my back. I could feel the weight of it pressing on my spine. My skin tingled. She'd told me about ancestor spirits, but for sure she didn't *believe*, did she?

'Did you see it too?' I asked.

Kate looked blank. 'See what?'

'The eagle …'

But I didn't say any more. She hadn't seen the eagle. She was talking about some guy.

'Did you ever wonder why you were brought such a long way to a place of safety?' she said.

I hunched my shoulders. I couldn't keep up with her today, the way she kept changing the subject.

'I figured no one else'd have me.'

Kate smiled. 'Children aren't brought halfway across Canada for no reason, Terry.' She gave me that bright, curious look of hers. 'Remember I told you how the first thing they'd done when you were taken in was to trace your family? Well, they traced your father.'

I thought of the eagle again. *They'd traced him. I'd seen him.* 'Hey, remind me to visit his grave sometime.'

'Terry, he's not dead.'

Dumb. So fucken dumb.

'He's living in Vancouver. That's why you were brought here. To be near to him.'

I slammed my fist on the beach. One of the stones sliced my hand.

'My father is dead!' I shouted.

Kate shook her head. 'Your father is alive.'

I scrambled to my feet, trying to ignore her. 'Quit doing this. It's not funny.'

'I'm not laughing, Terry.'

I started backing away from her down the beach. She got up too, and reached out to me.

'He wants to see you, Terry.'

'NOOOO!'

The rocks tossed the sound back at me. **NO!** NO. No …

I swung at Kate, but my eyes fogged up and my fist soared harmlessly through the air. I skinned my knuckles again on the shingle, steadying myself. Then I ran.

It took a second for Kate to figure where I was headed. I heard her footsteps behind me, slipping and sliding over the shingle.

'Terry, don't be so bloody stupid!'

But I was already ankle deep in the water, pushing the canoe out into the lake. As I jumped in, I saw Kate lunge for the stern. She missed, and must have fallen, because there was a big splash. I glanced back once over my shoulder and saw her scramble to her feet, a red rose of blood blooming on her leg.

I drove the paddle in too deep and the canoe lurched over the water. I paddled till my hands got too big to hold the paddle. The last time the blade hit the water, my fingers lost their grip. I watched the shaft cartwheel out of my hands and sink below the surface of the water. And I folded up like a jackknife.

I crouched for a long time, my eyes on the stained white bottom of the canoe. My knuckles were smarting and the cut on the side of my hand was starting to throb. A wind blew over my soaking wet shirt, and I shivered in the hot sun. I made a bargain with myself. If I looked up and saw the eagle, then Kate was lying and my father was looking out for me. But if the eagle was gone, then Kate was telling the truth, and my father was alive.

I straightened myself out and looked up. I scanned the sky. Once. Twice. Three times. But the eagle was gone.

My father was alive.

But if he's alive, he could have come for me. And he never did.

Away in the distance I heard the stutter of a small outboard motor. Over my shoulder I saw a rubber dinghy pull away from the jetty. Kate must have scared up some help.

The little boat bounced over the water, moving fast, growing bigger as I watched. I turned my back. I thought it would turn off to rescue Kate, but I could hear it coming on, past the island.

I kept staring into the green waters of the lake. Into the upside-down world. Maybe that's where I belonged. Maybe I'd find a reflected eagle who'd shed his eagle feathers and claim me as his son. Maybe that's where I'd be safe.

The dinghy engine sounded real close. I pitched back, and the canoe rocked beneath me. Icy water splashed my hand where it gripped the side.

The guy was near enough that I could see his ginger hair poking out from under his cap, the rash of pink freckles across his face. He looked like this wasn't where he was fixing to be today. His walkie-talkie crackled and he picked it up. Whatever it said, he didn't like it. He set his hand to the tiller, and the dinghy wheeled away in a half circle and came to a rest a hundred yards away, its engine idling.

For a few seconds it was standoff. Me in a canoe that was threatening to roll, him with his hand on the tiller, waiting to sweep in and fish me out of the water. Slowly, I straightened up, the canoe steadied itself, and the dinghy settled itself down in the water to wait.

I shut my eyes.

I tried to think about the dad I'd dreamt of as I lay in the bottom of my den. The father who was going to teach me all I needed to know. Who was going to protect me and make me strong.

But all I could see was the dad that Ed had made. The dirty, drunken, good-for-nothing Injun. The one who was sweeping the streets. Or shuffling from garbage can to garbage can, scavenging in the white man's trash.

The one who never came. No matter how hard I called.

So why should I care if this piece of Injun trash was alive or dead?

Because he was half of me, that's why. The half that Ed had tried so fucken hard to beat out of me all those years.

I needed to meet him face to face. Just once. To find out what it was that dragged me down.

I needed to look the worst part of myself in the eye.

The second paddle was still under the thwarts. And so were the lifejackets. I turned the canoe round and looked back towards the island. It was a long way away. Two, maybe three times as far as we had paddled that morning. I could make out the stick figure of Kate, white against the charcoal grey of the beach.

I was in big trouble, for sure. Maybe enough trouble to test Kate's crazy promise. But I figured that even if she was gonna kick me out, she'd feed me first. And I was very, very hungry.

I reached forward and pulled out one of the life jackets, and tied it on the way I had been taught. Then I started paddling back towards the island, my rubber dinghy escort following me at a safe distance.

Kate was on the grey shingle beach, arms hanging stiffly by her sides. One sleeve of her white shirt had been torn off and tied round her leg in a crude bandage. Her face looked about as white as her shirt, and I wondered how much blood she had lost.

I paddled the canoe the last few yards into the bay. Kate waded out into the water and helped to pull it up onto the shingle. As I stepped out, she reached up to put her arms round me, and I found I was shaking all over. Together we stumbled up the beach to where it was dry. Kate wrapped a blanket round my shoulders, and sat beside me with her arms around me.

'It's okay?' I mumbled, confused. 'You're not mad at me? You're not going to send me away?'

Kate made a sound that was somewhere between a sob and a laugh. Kneeling in front of me on the stones, she put her hands either side of my face and tilted it up.

'Terry, I'm so angry with you I'd have you clapped in irons and … *court-martialled* if I could. But I'm not going to send you way. Dammit, I'm not going to let you out of my sight.'

She put her arms round me again and kissed the top of my head—which goes to show I was right all along. She was crazy.

We went back in the rubber dinghy, the canoe trailing behind like the tail of a kite. The guy with the freckles was a doctor, Kate said. She insisted I let him check me over, to make sure I hadn't done myself any harm. He didn't say a whole lot—just bandaged up my hand and told her to see that I rested.

Kate must have meant what she said about not letting me out of her sight, because that night she sat in the chair beside me as I was going off to sleep. It was strange having someone in the room with me. Like my mom used to sit sometimes when Ed had gone out. He'd always go out after he'd belted us. Sometimes for days. And my mom would sit in my room and stroke my head, and wait for me to go to sleep.

Why didn't she pack up and go? When she knew he wasn't coming right back? Why did we always stay and wait for the next time?

Kate hadn't said a word. Not about my dad. Not about me going off in the canoe like that. I tried to think about how I would draw her. Red chalk with a sepia wash maybe. Not too much detail, just what I could see in this half light …

Jeez. Hell. I wish she'd say something. Then I wouldn't have to be mad at myself. Then I wouldn't have to be the one to say it first.

Jeez.

'You knew about my dad all along?'

Kate turned her face towards mine. I could see the smudged lines that made up her profile.

'Yes,' she admitted.

'Why didn't you tell me?'

Her hand came up and touched the space between her eyebrows.

'I tried. But every time I started to talk to you about him, you shut down. You were so sure he was dead. I had to wait until I thought you were ready to hear he was alive.'

I didn't feel ready.

'And this guy says he wants to see me?'

'Yes.'

'Why?'

'Because you're his son.'

I turned towards the wall and buried my face in the pillow. *That wasn't enough. It had never been enough.*

'If he cared so much about that why didn't he come? All those times I called him?'

I heard Kate draw breath, as if I'd finally surprised her. 'When? When did you call him?'

'Every time Ed belted me,' I answered, through a mouthful of pillowcase. 'I called him to come and take us away. But he never came.'

Kate blew out again—one long slow breath. Her hand touched my shoulder where it jutted from the duvet. 'Whatever happened to make him go, your father left you and your mother in safe hands. He had no reason to think you were in any danger.'

I rolled over, and my ear found a damp patch on the pillow.

'So why'd he never check on us?'

Kate took my hand between hers. Her palms felt dry, and cooler than they had under the hot sun.

'We all do things, with the best of intentions, that turn out to be the worst things that we could possibly have done.' She ran the tip of her tongue over her lips like she was having difficulty getting the words out. 'Nothing we do can change the past. We can only live with what we've done.'

I took my hand out of hers and turned away, studying shadow patterns on the wall.

'You're not just trying to get rid of me?'

Kate pulled the white cover thing—a duvet, she called it—up over my shoulder. 'For as long as you need it, you have a home here. Now go to sleep.'

The half-light had deepened into shadow. Kate was a deeper mass of shadow against the wall. I thought she'd gone to sleep, but every so often I heard her shifting a little in the chair.

'I don't want him to come here,' I said.

'Who?'

Kate's voice in the dark sounded startled.

'My father. I don't want my father here.'

There was a long silence.

'Do you want me to take you to Vancouver?' she asked.

'Okay,' I said. And went to sleep.

Chapter 9

The building had a glass elevator running up the inside.
I could see it, scuttling up the side of what Kate called an atrium, stopping to spew out the people it had gobbled up on other floors. From inside that thing, I was gonna be able to see out.

Jeez, I was gonna be able to see *down*.

I wiped my palms on the seat of my pants. Kate looked at me.

'I could phone up and ask him to come down,' she said.

I shook my head grimly.

The glass cab crawled to a stop in front of us. Panels on its belly slid back, and two men in suits stepped out.

'Sure?' Kate said.

My teeth were too tightly clenched to say anything. I stepped in, turned round, and held onto the rail as hard as I could.

It was a second before I realized the thing was moving. My stomach tried to squeeze out through the soles of my runners, then shot past where it should be, had a go at coming out of my ears and finally flopped back into place just as the doors opened.

'You okay?' Kate asked.

I nodded. I wasn't sure my legs were going to work, but one shifted in front of the other.

'I think it's this way,' she said.

I followed her towards an open door. The corridor smelled of wood and polish and fresh coffee. My feet sank into soft carpet. I'd given up trying to figure what my dad was doing in a place like this. Someone was going to explain what we were doing here. Some time.

At the end of the corridor, Kate moved aside let me go first. I stepped through a door—and stopped as if someone had put a hand in the middle of my chest. All I could see was a face, staring out from the wall opposite the door.

It was huge face, like maybe a yard high. A black and white photograph of an Indian, real old, like fifty or sixty. His hair hung down in two long braids. No feathers or beads or anything. Just an ordinary lumberjack shirt.

He was looking up at something, but you couldn't see what because his face filled the whole picture. He had wide eyes, kind of hooded. High cheekbones. Chin square and stubborn looking. Nose like a beak.

My face. The face I looked at in the mirror every morning.

I ran my fingers over my skin, half expecting it to be lined and wrinkled like the face in the picture. Grained, like a piece of carved wood. The grey braids of hair look pale in the photograph. Lighter than the skin. Skin that was the colour of Auntie Jean's strong tea …

Holy jeez.

Kate stared at the photograph. There was a man in the room too—an ordinary, human-sized man—and the man stared at me, the colour coming and going in this face.

'If there was ever any doubt,' Kate began, 'that you were who … or that we were …'

'Who *is* that?' I whispered.

He looked over his shoulder toward the photograph.

'Terry, that's your grandfather.'

He stood behind a desk. A big man, over six foot tall, starting to put on weight. Dark hair, kind of short. He was wearing a suit, and an old-fashioned tie. And he had the cleanest hands I'd ever seen.

'Hello, son,' said the man.

A name plaque stood on the desk right by where those clean, clean hands were resting. It said, 'JOSEPH HAVELOCK'.

Uh uh. No way. This wasn't him. Just because he had dark hair and a suntan and my name on the desk and a picture of me on the wall didn't make him my dad. He didn't even look like an Indian.

He started to talk with me, smiling and smiling like his mouth was stuck that way. I didn't say a word. I kept looking at the photograph. He wasn't whoI'd come for—this man in a suit, in a big office. But I had to find out what my face was doing up there.

The man's voice ran down like a wind-up toy. Before the silence could snap tight, Kate said, 'Shall we go and get a drink? Talk somewhere else?'

Aw, fuck.

'Do we have to go back down in that elevator thing?' I said to her.

'You hate it too, eh?' The man in the suit butted in. I gave him a look that ought to have shrivelled him up.

'I thought Indians were supposed to be these real great climbers?'

He spread his hands and I saw again how clean they were, the nails carefully shaped, like little spades. 'I think that's the Mohawk,' he said.

'Yeah? And I guess you're not Mohawk?'

He touched his fingers to his chest. 'We're Haida. From the islands off the Northwest Pacific Coast.'

His smile was sure beginning to bug me. 'So what are they?' I said. 'Some kind of fishing Indians?'

'Fishermen,' he nodded. 'Whale hunters. Sea-faring

warriors.'

We waded back through the thick carpet to the elevator doors. The elevator came and I didn't want to talk any more. The man went pale on the way down too, and nobody said anything till we reached the bottom.

Outside, it was hot. Late summer, late afternoon heat. Kate bought some ice cream and we walked towards the sea. The man who said he was my father kept talking, and Kate walked beside him, listening. I trailed behind, licking away at my ice cream. Every now and again, the man turned back, trying to include me. But Kate would lay a hand on his arm, like she was warning him to ease off, and on they'd go again.

We reached a beach crowded with sunbathers. Kate kicked off her shoes, and so did the man in the suit. When I took off mine, the sand burned my toes.

The man took off his jacket and fanned himself.

'We don't often get it this hot,' he said.

They started off across the sand, and I followed. Honey-coloured sunlight oozed over the beach, and the air above the sand shimmered. The heat was making me feel weird. The face on the wall in the office filled my head, and for a time it seemed like I was that old Indian, and I was remembering my younger self walking across the sand, following Kate and the man.

They reached a spot away from the swimmers and the volleyball players and the sunbathers. The man sat on a piece of driftwood, his legs apart, his bare feet planted in the sand. I squatted on the sand a little way away from him. I could see the high cheekbones in that jowly face, the wide eyes dragged down in the corners.

I made an oval in the hot sand with my finger, and as a kind of reflex added eyes and nose and mouth. The face became the face in the picture. The old Indian, looking up at something you couldn't quite see.

A man like that, with money and a suit and an office—if he was my dad, he could have come for me anytime he wanted. So wouldn't that mean he just didn't fucken care?

The face smiled.

Just because he has your picture, I told it, *doesn't make him my dad. Doesn't prove anything.*

I kicked away the picture in the sand. But its voice lingered. *He knows about me, though,* it said. *He can tell you who I am.*

'So what's he looking at?' I said.

'Who?' The man looked startled, like he'd forgotten I had a voice.

'That man in the photograph.'

'Your grandfather?' The man raised his hand, miming something tall. 'He is standing by a totem pole that he carved, just after it was raised.'

'A totem pole? For real?'

My head tipped back, imagining the pole standing in the sand.

The corner of the man's eyes creased up. I could tell he was getting a kick out of my amazement. 'I have another copy of the photograph at home. You can see the whole totem pole, and your grandfather standing next to it. I have other things he carved too.'

'Other totem poles?'

He shook his head. 'Smaller things. Masks, boxes and stuff.'

I stared at the sand, trying to imagine what it would be like to turn the pictures in my head into carvings in wood instead of pictures on paper. To feel the shape and the weight and the texture of them, to hold them in my hands. I tried shaping some sand between my feet, but it was too dry even for kids' sandcastles. I wriggled my toes, and it flowed away.

'They say in the old days that the woodcarvers were some of the most respected men in the tribe,' the man said, 'next to the chief in importance. Your grandfather came from a long line of artists.'

A long line of artists … Then I did too. It was in my blood …

'He got a name?'

The man nodded. 'He was Theodore Havelock. The same as you. But he was also He Who Captures the Raven.'

'Raven?' I'd seen ravens once or twice up in the mountains, ink black against the white of the snow. It didn't exactly sound like an artist's name. 'Why a raven?'

'It was his clan bird.' He saw I didn't get it and he sat up, cupping air in his hand, beating out time like a teacher in front of a class. 'The Haida are all members of two clans—the Ravens and the Eagles. You always married outside your own clan. And the children belonged to the clan of the mother.' He held his hands out sideways to include me in. 'Your grandfather was of the Raven clan. I am an Eagle, like my mother. And you—if you were part of the tribe, you would be a Raven too.'

Hey, I used to imagine you as an eagle, I thought. But I pushed the idea away. This wasn't my dad. I wasn't buying that. No way.

Chapter 10

He told us we were welcome to come up to his weekend cottage and see the things my grandfather had made. I didn't want him getting any ideas, like I believed he was my father or anything. But I wanted to see those carvings. So I said it would be okay.

Kate drove us up there the next day. The cottage was surrounded by trees, so the sun came through speckled, with the heat taken out of it. The man—Joseph—was standing on the porch waiting for us. Not in a suit today but in a light check shirt, like a summer version of the one in the photograph.

The cottage was tidy inside, like the cabin of a ship. The thing you noticed first was all the stuff hanging on the walls. Old photographs of Indians and Indian villages. Strange drawings in black and white and ochre. Carved wooden masks.

The first thing he showed me was a Raven mask, carved out of red cedar wood. It smelled like the chips they used to put down in the play park back home.

'The Raven was the bringer of light to the world,' he told me. 'He stole light from a box and placed it in the sky to make the sun. But he was a trickster, a mischief-maker—always getting into trouble.'

I wanted to touch it. I figured you weren't supposed to, like in a museum. But Joseph held it out for me to take. My fingers moved over the painted surface. I could feel the small marks my grandfather's tools had left in the wood.

'He's dead, right?'

Joseph nodded. 'He died three years ago.'

Three years. I turned it over in my hands. The shape was strange, not like any white person would have carved. *Three years ago I could have touched the hands that made this.* The tools would have left their marks there too, wearing patterns of calluses onto his palms, his fingers.

'It's something, eh?' said the man.

He was squatting beside me, legs wide apart, feet flat on the floor. Most folks squatted on the balls of their feet, their calves cramping under the strain. I'd never seen anyone else squat like me before.

He pointed up at a photograph on the wall.

'There's your grandfather with his totem pole.'

And there he was again. The old Indian with my face. Tiny next to the pole he had carved.

'That's the Raven,' Joseph pointed with his index finger. 'At the top of the pole. You see the sun disk in his mouth?'

The pole seemed to stake the old man to the ground, rooting him to the earth he shared with his ancestors. *Our ancestors.*

'What happened to it?'

'The pole? It's still on the island. For now.'

'Whatcha mean, for now?'

'The loggers are coming,' he said. He sounded calm, like he'd deal with that problem when the time came. 'Our people may not be able to stop them.'

My hands curled into fists. I thought about the pole uprooted, torn down. The Raven turned to wood chips, maybe. It was like being given a present and having it taken away before I could even open it. What if I never got to see it? Touch it?

The man touched my arm, his fingers resting on my sleeve. 'Something else you should see.'

I pulled myself away from the photograph and saw he was pointing to a carved blanket box standing against the wall.

'You know what's special about these boxes?'

I shrugged, and the man's eyes crinkled. He opened up the lid, and a smell of cedar wood filled my nose.

'They made them all of one piece. See?' He showed me the corner of the box where the wood was bent at right angles. 'They made these partial cuts in the wood and they'd steam it until it would bend into four sides. Then they'd peg the fourth corner, and the base.' He turned it so I could see. 'Our people never used pottery. They didn't need to. They could make boxes like these so perfectly watertight they used them for cooking pots, water buckets—everything.'

He shut the lid again and I saw the rounded square of a face carved in the front. My finger moved over the sweeping curve of the eyes, the short, down-thrusting triangle of the beak. There was something on the wings I couldn't make out, like another face.

'The Raven?' I asked.

He nodded. 'Your grandfather carved the Raven into everything he did.'

'Like a trademark?'

'Kind of. But it was much more than that. More like breathing a little part of his soul into the wood.' He sat back on his heels again. 'He used to say the artist must be a Trickster, like the Raven. He has to trick the wood into giving up its secrets and play tricks in people's minds to make them see the things he sees. If he's lucky—once in a lifetime—he will bring the gift of light to the world.'

The corners of his mouth curled, and his eyes held mine. I reached out and touched the beak of the Raven. *Bringer of light to the world.* I closed my eyes and let my fingers feel the shape of the wood.

Could you be a Raven, painting on paper as well as carving in wood? Maybe you could. There were drawings on the walls too. Drawings of animals mostly. When Joseph went to make coffee, I prowled round the room studying them. Some of the animals

I could guess at—I figured a Raven, and maybe a whale—but some of them, I hadn't a clue. It was like the artist had tried to draw everything he knew in his head, whether he could see it or not. The strangeness of them, the *rightness* of them, made the hairs on the back of my neck prickle.

Joseph was in the kitchen. I could hear him filling the kettle. Kate was out on the porch, watching woodpeckers in the trees. On a coffee table in the corner I saw a picture in a little silver frame I hadn't noticed before. I turned it round, thinking I was going to see another drawing.

It was Mom.

I felt burning. Starting in my prick and spreading. Down my legs. Up my arms …

What the fuck is this bastard doing with a picture of my mom?

She was leaning on the arm of a man. Leaning on his arm and laughing. A young man with a broad, slightly flattened face, and eyes that dragged down a little in the corners. A man with short, dark hair and skin the colour of Auntie Jean's strong tea …

I heard a chink of cups. I turned and he was standing at the kitchen door, tray in his hands, coffee cups balanced.

So it was true. This Joseph character was for real. He was my dad, the man I'd come to face.

I hurled the picture at him across the room. It hit the wall in front of him and shattered. Glass sprayed out, falling like a shower of rain, on the tray, on the floor, over his shoes.

My father stared open mouthed, still holding the tray out in front of him.

'You abandoned us!' I yelled. 'You let him go on hurting us. You should have protected us. You never protected us.'

Fireworks exploded on the backs of my eyelids. My father moved towards me. Then the porch door opened and I saw Kate shake her head urgently and wave him away.

'Terry.'

Her face was very close.

'Do you hear me?'

He never came. He never came. He never came.

'Terry?'

I shuddered and blinked, and focused my eyes on hers. She waited a moment till she was sure I was with her.

'Terry, you have the right to ask your father anything you like,' she said, 'and tell him anything you like. But not the right to attack him. Not the right to wreck his home.'

I oughta kill him for what he did. I oughta …I oughta …

Kate's hands weighed down on my shoulders, bringing me back.

'You don't have to like him, Terry. You don't have to love him. You don't have to call him Dad. But you do have to listen to what he has to say. Even when it hurts. Otherwise what are we doing here?'

My hands fluttered up, trying to push away her words, then fell back, dropping in my lap.

'You feel what you feel,' she went on more gently. 'No one can take that away from you. But he has rights too, Terry.'

I slumped a little, and she put her arms around me. I felt my anger earth through her.

'We can get back in the car and drive to Vancouver and catch a plane back to Achmore, if that's what you want. And you'll never have the answers to your questions.' She ran a hand over my hair. 'Or you can hold your head up high and you can go out there and you can talk to him.' She brought my hands up to her chin. 'It's up to you.'

A shudder ran through me again, and she hushed me.

The porch door was open. Outside, the man who really was my father paced up and down under the trees. I stood for a minute in the shadow of the porch. Behind me, I could hear Kate sweeping up the shards of broken glass.

I climbed down the three steps from the porch. As I reached the bottom step, he saw me, and quit pacing. I wanted to go back, but my feet carried me on.

'So if you're from out here on the Pacific,' I asked, my voice sounding like it was being squeezed from a blocked pipe, 'how come I got born outside Montreal?'

'You weren't. You were born out here in B.C.'

He hadn't always been a big hotshot lawyer. Back then, he'd been the most junior associate, and the only native lawyer in the firm. 'One day an Anglo girl from Quebec came to work as a secretary in our office.'

'She worked out here? In B.C. Uh uh. My mom didn't work. She didn't leave home. She was sick.'

The smile stayed on his face but I watched it leach out of his eyes. 'Not back then,' he said. He sat down on a fallen log and flicked some lint from the leg of his pants. 'Back then she could light up a room just by walking into it. She had more energy than all the rest of the office put together.'

He looked up, red eyed. *Crocodile tears.*

I turned my back on him. 'What did you do to her?'

'I ... fell in love with her. We got married. Then she got pregnant.'

'So whatever happened to happily ever after?'

'I wish I knew, Terry.' He motioned for me to sit beside him on the log, but I stayed where I was. 'I used to lie beside her on the bed, my hand on her belly, feeling the baby moving about inside her. Dreaming of the things we would do together.'

I squeezed my eyes shut and tried not to think how much I'd wanted that too.

Cute. Too bad you didn't stick around to try it.

'Something went wrong. After the birth, she was so sick. Not physically, exactly. She had what they call postnatal depression. It happens sometimes, after a baby is born. But usually it passes. The doctors kept telling us everything was okay, just give it time.' His head drooped like it had gotten too heavy for his neck. 'But it wasn't okay. It was like all the life had drained out of her. And she wasn't getting any better.'

Having a baby *did that too her?*

'What happened to the baby?' I breathed. But even as I said it, I knew the answer. Joseph reached for my hand and I didn't pull it away.

'It was you, Terry. You were the baby.'

The world swam. Pine needles crackled under my feet. A tree stood in front of me, its bark like broken tiles cemented together with pinkish gum. It swayed and I put out my hand to steady it. Tired, always tired, even before Ed had finished with her …

I did that to her. I made her sick.

'Terry?' My father's hand touched my shoulder and I rounded on him.

'So why did you go?' I yelled. 'Sick wife not in the deal? Was that it?'

'No!' He shook his head, his whole body denying it. 'Terry, I'd have done anything for her. For either of you.'

'Yeah. Right.'

'Maggie couldn't cope with a baby on her own. And I had to work. We didn't have any choice.' He closed his eyes for a moment, like he was tired or something. 'You and she went back to Quebec to live with your Auntie Jean.'

He slumped back onto the log.

'I couldn't afford to come every weekend. But I came as often as I could. I wanted to be the hero. I wanted to look after you both, to be the one to bring back the real Maggie.' He laughed without any humour. 'Your aunties started to tell me how she would pick up when I was away. How my visits would set her back. She'd make an effort while I was there, but afterwards she'd be in bed for days. Again and again, they told me how it would be better for her if I didn't come any more.'

He looked up into my face. Deep creases ran down from his eyes.

'You were nearly two the last time I came. I'd bought you a big box of crayons for your birthday.' He shrugged his big shoulders. 'I knew they wanted someone to blame. Problem was, I'd started to believe it was true, that I was making things worse for her. If I left, Maggie would get well again and you would be taken care of.'

He waited for me to speak, but I had nothing to say to him. Somewhere, away in the woods, a hammering sound began. It rose to a frantic peak and died away. I saw a flash of red, high up against the needle blackness.

'You couldn't have checked up on us?' I said, in the sudden silence.

He stared down at the forest floor, his hands on his knees like he was stopping them from shaking.

'The family convinced me that a clean break would be best,' he said. 'After the divorce, I moved apartments, buried myself in work. None of them even had my address.'

'But you had ours?'

'Yes, I had yours.'

'And you never thought to find out how we were?'

'I thought of it. All the time. Every Christmas. Every birthday. I wondered what your face looked like. How your mom was. But I'd made myself believe the best way to keep you both safe and well was to stay out of your lives.'

I swallowed hard, choking on a lump the size of a pinecone.

'You sure got that wrong, didn't you?' I said.

'Yeah,' he said. He held out his hand again. 'I sure did.'

It was the start of fall. I'd been back and forth to visit Dad a few times. He took me to the Canucks' first game, and Henri Richard led the Habs out onto the ice for the first time. And now Dad had brought me here, to the island of the Haida, where my grandfather had carved his totem poles. Today, on the last day of our visit, fog had rolled in off the ocean and the thick boles of the pine trees grew up out of a watercolour wash of greys. I shrugged my sweater closer round me and kept walking, following the line of trees along the shoreline.

Not just pine trees. My father had taught me that. Cedar, of course. And Sitka spruce. Hemlock. He'd shown me how each one had different bark, different needles. But none of them were changing with the coming winter. No bright colours. Not like the fall back east.

'No maple trees here,' he'd said, when I asked him. 'They don't grow out west.'

'They grow in Achmore,' I said, thinking of the leaf that had blown against the window, that day back in spring when I told Kate about the maple leaf belt buckle.

'They must be planted. Not native.'

Today I was on my own, exploring. My feet sank into the spongy carpet of moss that covered everything that wasn't a permanent track. Down below me, I could hear the waves rolling up the beach and tumbling back down again. But the edge of the ocean was hidden in fog.

Every few yards I heard another sound. The snap of a twig, maybe. Or the *ouf* of breath let out in a rush. I couldn't shake the feeling I was being followed. But when I stopped, there was nothing. Ghosts in the forest, that's all.

My grandfather's totem loomed ahead, its Raven flying clear of the trees at the edge of the old village. Most days you could see it easily from the wharf where they launched the fishing boats. But today I was nearly on top of it before I caught sight of it.

It wasn't alone. Five or six other poles stood in a loose semicircle, a little to one side. Their paint had worn away. I touched one of them and my finger left a dent in the soft cedar wood. One of them leaned crazily, its base rotted to pulp. One more lay at an angle on the ground, half covered in moss—held in shape by force of habit, I guess.

The poles were meant to be left like this, the Haida said. To return to the soil. But sometimes, when the wind was in the right direction, I could hear the logging machines working away to the north. That was different. That wasn't meant to happen.

I felt in my rucksack for the sketch pad and the box of Conte crayons that Kate had given me. The thick watercolour paper was growing damp in the fog. When I started to draw, it changed the look of the pastilles. The crayon went on smooth, leaving a deeper colour. I wet my finger and rubbed at it, and the line softened. One colour bled into the next.

I can do something with this.

I worked on, letting the fog change the surface of the paper, trying things out, experimenting. Once or twice I dragged the crayon too hard and damaged the surface of the paper. But Kate's big block of paper gave me freedom. I could make mistakes, start over. I wasn't going to run out for a long time.

The first tug at my sleeve I barely noticed. I thought my sweater had caught on something and I tugged back. It tugged again. Not a snag. Not a thorn. Something—*someone*—pulling me back.

A boy from the village stood beside me. He was about four years old, his hair pulled back in a ponytail. His clothes looked like someone bigger had worn them first.

He'd ripped me from the dream I'd been having. I could see the bleeding stump of it on the paper, still pulsing. For a second I imagined knocking the kid backwards, smashing his silly head on the rocks behind him. The thought made me shrivel inside, and I forced myself to look at his face.

He was staring up at my head, his hands on his hips.

'Why's your hair so short?' he demanded.

For a second my brain freewheeled. 'The bogeyman got me,' I told him, when I'd quit skidding.

'For real?' His eyebrows disappeared up into his hair. 'What's his name?'

'Ed,' I said. The name left a taste on my tongue. I wanted to spit. But the little kid fell on his back laughing, kicking his heels in the air.

'*Ed*. There's no bogeyman called *Ed*,' he spluttered.

'That's all you know,' I said, trying to sound menacing. He wasn't impressed. He scrambled to his feet and wriggled round to get a look at my drawing.

'You drawing the totem pole?' he asked.

'I was *trying* to.'

'Can I see?' he persisted.

'No.'

He thrust a piece of paper towards me.

'See. I drawed it too.'

I blinked. I could see something drawn in bright crayon. A kid's drawing.

'That's pretty good,' I said, with an effort. 'You like to draw?'

He nodded hard. 'I drawed all the time.' He pointed to something at the top of the page. Two eyes. 'That's the Raven, see? Like me. Mikey. I'm a Raven.'

'That right?' I gave a half smile. 'I'm a Raven too.'

'Yeah?'

I pointed to the totem. 'My grandfather carved that,' I told him.

That set him off giggling again. 'No, silly. My grandpa carved it. Don't you know anything?'

Another cousin, then.

'You know the story of the Raven?' I asked, to distract him.

'Which one?'

'The one where he steals the light from the box.'

'Everyone knows that one,' he answered.

'You tell it me.'

So Mikey told me the story. It was muddled up and upside down. He had to go back and fit bits of it back in. But sometimes you could hear he was telling the story the exact same way his mom or his dad or his grandpa had told it to him, and the way their grandpas told them, and their grandpas before that.

I started to draw. I drew shadows of the story behind the poles. Ghosts in the fog. Echoes. Not what I saw, but what I knew in my head. It wasn't right. But it was the closest I'd got.

When he'd done telling the story, Mikey got bored. He wandered away, with a 'see ya' and a wave of his hand. Back down the way I had come, a jay flew up, cawing a warning. Voices came to me, carried oddly by the fog.

'Hi … Uncle Joe.'

'… Mikey. Your mom's … for you.'

'Better be … then …'ya.'

My dad appeared, a denser patch in the fog.

'I think you made a hit there,' he said as he came close. 'Mikey's pleased as all get out to have another artist look at his drawings.'

I shrugged. 'He's a nice kid, I guess.'

'He's your cousin, you know.'

'Yeah, I figured.' I ran my hand through my hair. 'Sometimes it seems like I'm related to everyone around here.'

My dad laughed. 'You probably are, just about.'

'I can't get the hang of it.'

'It'll come.' He sat down on the boulder next to me. I'd got used to the feel of his bulk near me. He didn't touch me much, but he liked to sit beside me, his feet planted on the ground, his hands on his thighs. 'That kind of brings me to what I was wanting to say.'

'Yeah?'

He took a deep breath of the fog and blew it out. 'I've been wondering how long you were thinking of sticking around?'

I shrugged and felt the fog in my sweater, clammy against my skin.

'You got to go away?' I asked.

He shook his head. 'Not yet a while.'

Instead of saying anything more, he stared off into the fog. His face was sort of screwed up, like he was fixing to say something difficult.

So this is it, I thought. He's going to send me away.

'Kate tells me you were in pretty bad shape when you first got to Achmore.'

'I guess.'

'You didn't speak for weeks ... after your mom's funeral.'

I hugged myself to get warm again. *What the hell are you getting at?*

'I can't begin to imagine—what you went through, watching her die.'

'You know what,' I said, with a sudden spurt of anger. 'Watching her die was a hell of a lot easier that watching her live.'

He put his hand on my shoulder. It made a patch of warm on my sweater.

'I'm sorry,' he said. 'I'm doing this all wrong. What I'm getting at is ... you went to Achmore because you needed help. Something more than just a home and a place to be safe.'

'I guess.' I shrugged again, and shivered.

'But ... I'm wondering if that has changed.'

'How do you mean?'

My dad looked me square in the face, like he'd come to a decision.

'I'm wondering if ... when you felt ready for it ... you'd think about coming to live with me.'

'What? Here, on the island?'

I hadn't seen it coming. My skin crawled, like he'd put bugs down my sweater. *Don't say it unless you mean it.*

'No, not on the island,' he answered. 'In Vancouver. But we could come here, if that was what you wanted.'

'What about when you went away?'

'I'd make sure I didn't. Not for a few years.'

'You said your work takes you all over the country, didn't you?'

'It has done,' he admitted. 'To Ottawa. That kind of thing. But

I'm old enough and ugly enough for that to be my choice. I don't have to take on those cases.'

I thought about all the stuff he'd shown me in the papers. The Cree, the Nisga'a …

'You told me lots of tribes are starting up land rights cases.'

He pulled down the corners of his mouth. 'Lots of lawyers are qualified to represent them. It doesn't have to be me. When it's time for the Haida to take a stand against the loggers, maybe I'll change my mind.' He leaned over and bumped shoulders. 'Until then, I reckon I can take a break without the world falling apart.'

I sat still for a long time. I thought, if he says anything, I'll have no space to think. But he stayed quiet.

So I thought about my mom, trapped inside the house that Ed built. Tired and sick because of me. Too sick to walk away. I thought about Kate, waiting for me in Achmore. I thought about my old den back in Montreal, about the hours I'd spent aiming imaginary arrows at the white kids that came to play, trying to be a warrior.

After all the searching, I'd found a place where everyone looked like me. A safe place.

A wind began to blow, softly at first. Ripples appeared in the fog, and slowly, slowly it began to retreat. And the rain came.

Chapter 12

Nearly Christmas. In Montreal it would have been snowing, or freezing, anyhow. According to Kate, there was already over a foot of snow in the mountains. Here in Vancouver, it was raining.

Dad and I were sitting at the breakfast bar, wrapping. We'd made French toast for breakfast, mixing the eggs and the milk and the cinnamon, dipping the bread, frying it. I could still smell the cinnamon, the hot oil, the eggs crisping.

A pile of newspapers lay on the counter in front of us, and all Dad's best dishes were out of the cupboard. In two days' time, Kate was flying in to undo the complicated legal knots that had made me her ward and hand custody to my dad. In a week's time we were moving to a new, two-bedroom apartment over in Burnaby where we wouldn't have to breathe in each time we passed each other. Then maybe I could start drawing again. Meanwhile, Dad and I were packing dishes.

I took a sheet from the Sports Pages. *The Habs, in their first season without big Jean Beliveau, are off to a flying start, unbeaten so far in the Eastern Division.* The Vancouver papers didn't follow the Canadiens like the *Gazette*, but they did cover their games. *New Captain, Henri Richard, led his team to a 4-3 victory over the Bruins at the Forum last night…*

'If you're going to read the whole paper before you wrap anything, I'll give you the money pages instead,' Dad grumbled.

But he winked, so I figured it was safe to ignore him. He picked up another bowl and a sheet of the funnies, but before he could finish wrapping, the buzzer sounded for the door.

'Be right back,' he said. I scooched up to let him past and his hand ruffled its way through my hair. 'Don't go breaking anything while I'm gone, eh?'

Dad let the visitor come up. It was a guy I'd seen before, a partner from Dad's law firm. He was shaking his wet raincoat and waving a big manila envelope.

'I figured you ought to see this one, Joe.'

'C'mon in, Harv.'

Dad led Harv into his study. I couldn't exactly hear their voices any more—only bits and pieces as their voices got louder. I carried on wrapping, reading anything I could find on the Habs, not paying attention, so what I heard was something like this:

'… biggest yet, Joe …'

'… told you my decision …'

… accurate passing by the Canadiens' winger in the second period …

'… asked for you specially …'

'Sure I'm honoured, but …'

… fed Richard on his glove side …

Their voices were louder. My dad was starting to sound angry, and I wondered what the other guy was saying to upset him.

'Jeez, it's Christmas, Harv!'

'I know it isn't the greatest time to ask you …'

… clean wrist shot from behind the blue line gave Montreal their third goal …

'Hell, Joe, you could get someone to look after the kid.'

I sat up, my heart thumping at my ears, and heard my father's thunderous, 'No!' I clung to the edge of the breakfast bar like it was a lifeline. For the first time I realised that there were currents that could drag me back into open water.

'… twelve years I've just about lived in our office …'

'Joe—'

'… been given a second chance. I won't throw it away.'

'We're talking the biggest case in aboriginal law in Canadian legal history. You can't turn it down!'

'I just did.'

I heard the *crrrk* of paper being torn, and their voices dropped away so I couldn't make out the words. The door to the study opened and Harv and my dad came out.

'I sure hope you'll reconsider,' Harv was saying.

The corners of Dad's eyes were dragged down more than normal. 'That's not going to happen.'

'No hard feelings?'

'No hard feelings.'

'Well, so long, Joe.' He glanced up at me. 'So long, kid.'

My mouth was dry. I mumbled, 'So long,' and he and Dad shook hands.

The door shut behind him and Dad came into the kitchen, straightening himself up as he came through the door.

'What did he want?' I asked.

'He wanted me to pick up a job.' His eyebrows flexed. 'Not this Christmas, eh?'

That night, when I was sure he was asleep, I crept off the camp bed and into Dad's study. The waste bin was pretty much empty. Just the manila envelope and the sheets of torn paper. I knew where Dad kept a flashlight.

There was a letter on creamy-white headed notepaper, and a bunch of legal documents about some Land Claim. The flashlight kept jerking about so it was hard to read, but I made out the gist of it …

```
'The council of elders of
the Cree Nation invite Joseph
```

> Havelock ... foremost practitioner
> in Aboriginal Law ... join a team
> of legal experts ... represent
> them in a case against the
> Provincial Government of Quebec
> ... protesting the plans for the
> James Bay hydroelectric project ...
> inevitable loss of a large area
> of tribal hunting grounds ...'

I shoved the envelope and the other papers back in the waste bin and hugged the torn pieces of the letter to me. I could feel my heart bumping against them under my pyjamas.

I started to shiver and I crept back under the blankets. I'd spent too long trying to keep myself awake. My eyes were on shutters. Harv's words and the words of the letter rolled through my head on waves of sleep. 'Joseph Havelock, foremost practitioner ...' 'The biggest aboriginal law case in Canadian legal history...'

Do you hear that, Ed? I yelled into the emptiness in my head. *That's your Indian trash, that is.*

It went on raining and raining. The day we were going to court to petition for the change of custody it rained so hard it seemed like someone had scooped up most of the Pacific Ocean and dropped it over Vancouver.

'We'd better get going early,' my father told Kate and me. 'The traffic downtown is brutal this time of day.'

On the way down in the elevator, my father put his arm around my shoulders.

'You okay, son?'

'Yeah. Pretty good.'

Outside you could have driven a submarine along the Trans-

Canada. The world went by in shades of grey streaked with colour. Bill boards. Shop fronts. Traffic lights. Other cars were points of light—receding red or advancing white. It was like someone had stuck their fingers in wet oil paint and dragged them across a canvas.

With nothing to look at, I shut my eyes. I could hear the rain drumming on the roof. Then it faded into the background. I began to hear the hiss of tires pushing through water. The beating of the windshield wipers. And the chitchat of my father and Kate. Content. Satisfied. Making ready for a conclusion.

The inside of the car felt like it was shrinking.

We slowed down at the approach to the Lion's Gate Bridge and crawled over it into Stanley Park. Dad's shoulders crept up towards his ears. Kate's finger rubbed the place between her eyes. There were long gaps in their talking.

'Good thing we left plenty of time, eh?'

Still six maybe seven blocks from the courthouse, my dad, on familiar territory, peeled off to the right to dodge the jam. The car speeded up. Arcs of water sprayed out on either side, gutter-yellowed water churned by our tires.

'I guess we're gonna get wet getting to the courthouse,' said Dad.

The car slewed a little in the standing water, and for a second Dad fought for control.

I was out of time.

'Stop the car,' I yelled.

'It's okay. I got it. It's not so bad.' Dad's voice was low, trying to be reassuring.

'Stop the car, will ya?'

'What is it, Terry?' Kate turned round to look at me over the back of the seat.

'You don't understand. Just stop the car. Please.'

Kate and Dad exchanged a look. I saw Kate dip her head, and Dad began to pull over, easing himself into the right hand lane. After a moment he turned into a parking lot by a mall and stopped the engine.

'Listen, son, if you're nervous about—'

'Shut up and listen, will ya?' My voice came out like the whistle on a steam kettle. The two of them sat silent, staring at me. My hands were shaking so much it took time to undo the buttons of my parka and feel in my pocket for the two torn pieces of paper. I thrust them towards Dad.

'You gotta tell Harv you changed your mind,' I said. 'You gotta take this job.'

Dad picked up the pieces of paper and looked from them to me as if he was struggling to remember what they were.

'Terry ...' His voice croaked and he cleared his throat. 'Terry, if I take this job, it won't just mean putting off your coming to live with me for a few weeks, or a few months. Cases like this can go on for years.'

'I know that.'

'Then why?' He stared at me, blinking like an owl woken in daylight. 'Don't you want to live with me?'

'Oh, jeez!' *Shaddup! Shaddup!* 'Kate, you promised me once. That I'd always have a home with you. No matter what ...'

She was staring at the pair of us, mouth open, lost. 'Yes, and I meant it, but—'

'What did you tell me? When I asked you why I should believe you?'

'I said ...' She closed her eyes. 'I said that it isn't just what I do, it's what I am.'

I smacked at the paper in Dad's hand.

'Well, that isn't what you do. It's what you are. And I'm not going to let you change that.'

'Terry ...' Dad opened his mouth and stopped, like he no longer knew what he wanted to say. His Adam's apple bobbed. 'Terry, this is my choice. You haven't forced me into it. It's what I want to do.'

Dad's hand squeezed mine too tight, and I pulled away. *I didn't figure it would be this hard.*

'Don't you get it?' I made myself angry so I wouldn't go spoiling things. 'All my life they've tried to make me ashamed of you. Well, I'm going to be proud of you. Of who you are. Joseph Havelock, 'foremost practitioner in aboriginal law'. Scoring a goal for the Cree Nation.'

Dad's face cracked. 'Terry, I'm not Jean Beliveau …'

'No, you're not. 'Cos I'm not going to fucken let you retire.'

Dad held up his hands and stared at Kate. In his eyes, the tide was beginning to turn. I could feel the current tugging at me, feel the wind in my face as he grew smaller and smaller. *Don't listen to me,* I wanted to shout. *What do I know? I'm just a kid.*

Dad got back into the car, blinking rain out of his eyes.

'I phoned the courthouse,' he said. 'Told them we were withdrawing the petition.'

Kate nodded.

Dad turned the car and headed back towards the bridge. The rain was easing. I could see the back of his neck over the seat in front of me. The thickening line over his collar. Tiny dark hairs growing where the barber shaved his old fashioned short back and sides. For the whole of the journey he never turned his head.

In the parking lot beside Dad's car, Kate hesitated. I reached towards her and she rested a hand for a moment in the small of my back.

'I think you two should have some time together,' she said, and she turned on her flat, sensible shoes and headed back towards the rental car.

My father and I went up in the elevator, standing as far apart as we could. The corridor leading to his apartment was half dark. He unlocked the door. When he flicked the light switch, the walls of the entrance hall lit up green, like light seen through leaves.

I stayed back in the half darkness. I watched my father take off his raincoat, open the louvered doors of the closet and hang it up inside. Packing cases were everywhere. Empty shelves. In the study, the carpet was rolled up.

Oh, jeez. I didn't mean to let you down.

'What are you going to do about the new apartment?' I said. And my tongue felt like a slab of raw meat between my lips.

He turned, his head lowered. I could see his short-cropped hair plastered to his head like wet paint.

'I guess I'm still going to need two bedrooms, eh?' he croaked. 'For when my son comes to stay?'

Dad came towards me and put his hands on my arms. And after a moment he drew me in, out of the dark, and shut the door behind me.

Thank you for reading a Triskele Book.

Enjoyed *Gift of the Raven*? Here's what you can do next.

If you loved the book and would like to help other readers find Triskele Books, please write a short review on the website where you bought the book. Your help in spreading the word is much appreciated and reviews make a huge difference to helping new readers find good books.

More novels from Triskele Books coming soon. You can sign up to be notified of the next release and other news here: **http://www.triskelebooks.co.uk**

If you are a writer and would like more information on writing and publishing, visit **www.triskelebooks.blogspot.com** and **www.wordswithjam.co.uk**, which are packed with author and industry professional interviews, links to articles on writing, reading, libraries, the publishing industry and indie-publishing.

Connect with us:
Email admin@triskelebooks.co.uk
Twitter @triskelebooks
Facebook www.facebook.com/triskelebooks

COMPLICIT

'On the beach stood the adverse array (of Britons), a serried mass of arms and men, with women flitting between the ranks. In the style of Furies, in robes of deathly black and with dishevelled hair, they brandished their torches; while a circle of Druids, lifting their hands to heaven and showering imprecations ...'

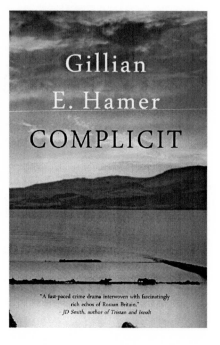

Gillian E. Hamer

COMPLICIT

"A fast-paced crime drama interwoven with fascinatingly rich echos of Roman Britain."
- JD Smith, author of Tristan and Iseult

When Roman historian, Cornelius Tacitus, recorded the invasion of the small island of *Mona Insulis* off the North Wales coast in 60AD – the beginnings of a propaganda war against the Druidic religion began.

Two thousand years later, that war is still being fought.

For two millennia, descendants of a small sect of Anglesey Druids have protected their blood lineage and mysterious secrets from the world. Until members of this secret society are murdered one by one.

Detective Sergeants Gareth Parry and Chris Coleman, along with new girl, DC Megan Jones, must stop this killer at all costs. What they discover will shock the whole police team and leave consequences which have an impact like no crime in the history of the force.

Set along the dramatic Menai Straits, *Complicit* is a story of greed, loss and obsession.

Also from Triskele Books

TREAD SOFTLY

"You don't attract trouble. You go looking for it."

Disheartened by her recent performance, Beatrice Stubbs takes a sabbatical from the Metropolitan Police for a gourmet tour of Northern Spain. In Vitoria, she encounters a distant acquaintance. Beautiful, bloody-minded journalist Ana Herrero is onto a story.

Beatrice, scenting adventure, offers her expertise. The two women are sucked into a mystery of missing persons, violent

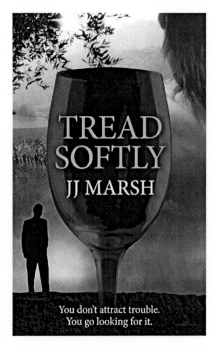

threats, mutilated bodies and industrial-scale fraud. They are out of their depth. With no official authority and unsure who to trust, they find themselves up to their necks in corruption, blackmail and Rioja.

Beatrice calls for the cavalry. The boys are back, and this time, it's a matter of taste. But when her instincts prove fallible, Beatrice discovers that justice is matter of interpretation.

TRISTAN AND ISEULT

In a land of fog and desperate tribes, Tristan fights to protect western Briton from Saxon invaders. In the wake of battle, he returns to Kernow bearing grave news, and the order of power shifts.

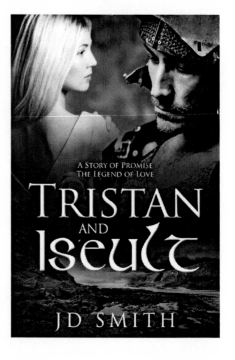

As Tristan defends the west, his uncle, King Mark, faces enemies to the east beyond the sea: the Irish Bloodshields. Mark is determined to unite the tribes of Briton and Ireland and forge an alliance that would see an end to war and the beginnings of peace.

Iseult, the daughter of Irish kings and a woman of the blood, resigns herself to her inevitable fate: marriage to Lord Morholt. A bloody duel changes her course, and she finds herself stranded on the coast of Kernow bringing with her the possibility of peace. But when she loses her heart to one man and marries another, her future and that of Briton flutters grey.

Three people and a hope that will never fade, this is a story of promise; the legend of love.

Lightning Source UK Ltd.
Milton Keynes UK
UKOW04f2206290415

250605UK00004B/201/P